Adventures of Abby Diamond

Author of the Month January 2009 in Sylvia McGrath's
Professor Owl's Newsletter and member of
Society of Children Book Authors and Illustrators

Adventures of Abby Diamond

Abby Diamond in Teenage Wizard and Secrets in the Attic

Kristie Smith-Armand, M.Ed, TVI

"It is a terrible thing to see and have no vision"
-Helen Keller

iUniverse, Inc.
New York Bloomington

iUniverse books may be ordered through booksellers or by contacting:

iUniverse
1663 Liberty Drive
Bloomington, IN 47403
www.iuniverse.com
1-800-Authors (1-800-288-4677)

ISBN: 978-1-4401-6626-6 (sc)
ISBN: 978-1-4401-6627-3 (ebook)

Printed in the United States of America

iUniverse rev. date: 9/22/2009

Thrills and Chills !!!

By: Jamille Smith

Abby Diamond's adventures are many,
Wherever she seems to roam.
She searches the past and the present
Whether near or far from home.

She experiences wars and a wizard,
(And once encountered a ghost!)
These glorious, exciting adventures
Are much more thrilling than most.

By searching for important clues,
And looking into some strange spaces,
Abby finds unsolved mysteries
In unexpected, chilling places.

She knows the natures of people,
Sensing meanings whatever they be.
Abby views situations more clearly
Than others are able to see!

So, come along with Abby Diamond!
Enjoy your trip through the pages.
Watch as she finds unknown answers
To questions down through the ages.

Dedicated to: Libby Daugherty, the real Abby
Jamille Smith, my mother and my muse
Richard Armand, my husband and muse
Karyn Cummings, my editor/sister
Shay Quinn, the real Neils
Yasmine Allen, my first Braille student

Abby Diamond
IN
Summertime Blues

"Meet Abby Diamond"

Hi! My name is Abigail Diamond, Abby for short, and even though I can't see, my friends and I love to solve the mysteries that are always finding their way to us. I live in a large house near one of my best friends, but that hasn't always been the case.

My dad has a great job now and works with my Grandmother Elizabeth's husband, Harry St. Claire, in computers. My Grandmother Elizabeth is my mother's mom and who is like me, blind. I actually inherited my eye condition from her.

Two of my other favorite people in the world are my dad's parents, Nan and Grand

Pop. They have been married for years and still act like teenagers.

Nan is a "Shop 'Til You Drop" kind of lady just like I am.

I also have a really cool sister named Katy who is married, a vision teacher now and a wonderful mother to my nephew, Brennan Jude. He's simply the cutest kid on the earth besides my own little brother, Chip. I actually nicknamed him Chip because he looks so much like my dad, Jacob.

My parents are great and loving but can be really strict which gets on my nerves.

Dad works hard at his computer job and my mom, Caroline, works part-time as a fifth grade teacher at my school.

From what people tell me, my mom is beautiful and looks just like my Grandmother Elizabeth. I am told that I look like them, too.

I saved the best part of my world for last. I have three of the best friends in the world: Neils, Alison and Andrea. Neils has long red curly hair and is what some people call a tomboy. After all, she is the only girl in the family besides her mother.

Alison is the daughter of a famous and rich movie star but she lives with the coolest dad on earth, Audie.

Audie isn't her blood father, but he has stepped into the role beautifully. Andrea lives by me in a really big house. Andrea has beautiful dark skin and large olive colored eyes from what Neils told me.

This is my life, and I wouldn't change one thing except for the fact that Jaxson is slowly becoming one of my favorite people. Just kidding! " Jaxson I wouldn't change that either."

"The End of the School Year"

When I was younger, I always loved the end of the school year, but not like I do now. I'm much older and more mature except for the fact that I still sleep with my favorite blanket.

"Hey, Glen, you want to go see that new movie that is scaring the dickens out of people," Jaxson asked his copycat friend.

"Heck, yes," was Glen's surprise answer.

Jaxson could say that the sky was green or that ice cream was sour and Glen would agree. After all, Jaxson was Glen's only friend, and he wasn't about to lose him.

"Gross," Alison said, "I have better things to do with my time than watching some scary movie," she snorted.

"Me, too," I agreed and hoped my voice wasn't giving me away. I mean I am known for my courage, but not when it comes to movies that give you nightmares.

"Abby, do you go to the movies?" Dumb-Dumb Glen asked.

"Yes, Glen," I moaned along with my buddies, Neils, Andrea and Alison.

"I have ears, you dope," I answered. "There are many ways to 'see' things, Glen."

I had to bite my tongue before I called him a long list of names.

"Huh," was all "Goofy" Glen added.

"Hey, come on, Girl," Neils blasted. "LET'S GO AND SEE THAT FLICK."

"Like I told Glen, Neils, I still have my hearing."

I was trying to avert the conversation because I did not want the gang to know that I was frightened to death of scary movies.

"Nightmares on Elm Street"

Okay, I don't really live on Elm Street, but I let Neils talk me into going to see one of the scariest movies ever. When Andrea and Alison agreed to go with her, I couldn't refuse; just forget the part about me being more mature.

The movie was all about ghosts that were chasing kids through the streets, calling them on their cell phones and talking to them through the internet.

Neils laughed her head off when Alison screamed a loud scream, then I screamed because Alison was screaming even though, thank goodness, I couldn't see the really scary parts.

"Hahahahha," Neils teased when we were finally leaving the theater. "That was so cool whenever that ghost grabbed that kid by the jacket and, blah, blah, blah," Neils described. I mean she described it over and over while we were waiting on my dad to pick us up from the theater.

"Neils, I don't believe in ghosts, so I am not scared at this silly made-up story. It was probably written by a boy in the first grade," I spewed.

"Keep telling yourself that, Abby," Neils teased.

On the way home in the car my stomach felt queasy from the hot dog, nachos, Whoppers and Coke that I consumed, so it wasn't helping me much when Neils began describing the blood and gore.

My stomach had had enough, and it was all Neils's fault.

"Dad, pull over," I yelled.

"What Abby?" he asked, but it was too late. My whole dinner was lying in the floor and all over Neils, and for the first time all night, she shut up.

"Vision Skills Program"

By morning Neils had forgiven me and even called to check on me.

"Abby are you okay?" she asked.

"I can sometimes get carried away when I describe movies. It drives my mother crazy," Neils said.

"Oh, sure, Neils," I added. "I am so sorry about my stomach getting all sick and everything. Hey would you like to go see the new Hannah Montana movie?" I asked.

"It has some really cool new songs, Rascal Flats, Taylor Swift and many other famous people."

Neils agreed, so Andrea, Neils, Alison and I went and saw the movie, but this time I stuck with drinking a coke and nothing else.

"Ooooh, I wanna be a rock star," Alison sang.

"Guys, Miley is a really cool kid in person," Alison told us and she should know. Alison has a great voice and since her mother is Kaitlyn Summers she has had the opportunities to show off her talent. She even sang once with Miley. I remember how sad she was though when she was in California with her rich, beautiful and famous mother singing.

"Alison, you really don't miss the life of a super star?" asked Andrea. "I mean, I want to be a super star one day and sing on American Idol and be like Fantasia or Carrie Underwood," Andrea dreamed.

"Ummm, no offense, Andrea," Neils spoke. "You are talented in many areas, but singing is not your thing," she added.

"What did you say?" Andrea joked and then tackled Neils on the grass.

We were all laughing and cutting up whenever I heard a voice come up from behind me. It was Sabre and she was with Josselyn and Esmeralda, three great girls that I knew from our Vision Skills Program.

"Hey, Abby," the girls said.

"Hey Sabre. Hey Josselyn and Esmeralda," I said and then introduced them to my buddies.

"I can't wait for the Vision Skills Program tomorrow," Sabre said.

"Me either," I added.

"I love when Mr. Tommy talks all serious to us. He is such a cool guy, and so are all of the teachers and O&M's at our program," I said.

"Do you remember last year when Mrs. Preston and Mrs. Gray started wrestling?" asked Josselyn.

"Yes, I cracked up," I laughed.

"Hey," I heard some kids call out.

It was a whole group of my summer school buddies: Gabrielle, Jimmy, sisters Jasmon and Passion as well as Ansley, Princess and

Sonia. We said good-by to my friends from Vision Skills Camp and wait for Neil's dad.

"Man, Abby," Neils began. "I wish I could go with you to the Vision Skills Program. I mean you guys get to go swimming, bowling, have races, and eat snacks all day."

"I wish y'all could be there with me, too," I added. However, I knew that as close as I am to my best friends, it's always good to have other friends, too.

"The Vision Skills Program"

The next morning it was time to go to the Vision Skills Program. I couldn't wait, so I didn't need my obnoxious alarm clock that crows and says, "2 am, 3am, etc."

"Abby, the bus is here," Mom yelled.

"Great, See ya, wouldn't want to be ya," I laughed. Chippy laughed too because he thinks that I am so cool, and he is correct. After feeling around, I climbed up the steps and sat down.

"Abby, come over here," Josselyn yelled.

"Hey, Josselyn, where's Sabre?" I asked.

"She's next on the pick-up."

After we picked up Sabre we talked nonstop until we got to the program.

"Okay," Mr. Tommy yelled. "Let's get settled and listen to the agenda for our program." I loved Mr. Tommy. He was a man who knew his business but he was always fun to be around.

While we were waiting on Mr. Tommy to begin his sermon, I mean speech, some more cool kids came up to me. Tyjahnae, Lakendra, Abigail, Michael, Jennifer, Carmen, Christina, Emmanuel, Jose and Kevin all gathered around me while Mr. Tommy began.

"This year," Mr. Tommy said, "We will study parts of history, work on reading and writing skills." We all moaned, and I moaned the loudest.

"Mr. Tommy. History is so boring," I said. "History?" he questioned. "Abby, history is one of the most important reasons for us being who we are today."

"Sure," we all mumbled.

"Kids, if it were not for men and women in history we would not have the freedom that we enjoy in the best and strongest country in the world. We would still be apart of England, or be broken into the northern and southern United States or be controlled by a mad man."

All of us were left speechless after Mr. Tommy got off of his pedestal.

We began the morning by taking a walk around the track after our stretches. Josselyn, Sabre, Ashley, Carmen, Esmeralda and I talked to Ms. Croom about hair and make up and junk. Ms. Croom was one of the Orientation and Mobility specialists who was young and fun.

"I just bought a really cool shirt that is a khaki color," she told us.

"Wow, what color is that?" Sabre asked. "Well have you ever had a butterscotch candy? It's similar to that color. Since you cannot see the color you can still understand what they are by using your other senses for the experience of colors," Ms. Croom said.

We walked around and were really enjoying ourselves when Mrs. Glover, another great O&M told us that we were now going to take a walk around the cemetery.

"Great," I whispered to Josselyn. "That is just what I want to do after seeing that crazy scary movie the other night."

"Abby, you don't believe in ghosts do you?" asked Sabre.

"Well, not really, but the idea of a cemetery really freaks me out." We laughed at my comment and slowly walked around the cemetery.

Another really cool kid named Jamil was walking with us as was Ernesto, Christina and Fernanda.

We were talking and cutting up with each other whenever we heard a kid yell,

"Who does that little girl belong to?"

"What little girl?" I asked.

"Look Ms. Croom," Josheph added. "Do you see her?"

"Yes," she added. "I do. She's about the size of an eleven year old and wearing a blue coat. It looks as though she is pointing at a tomb stone."

"Why is she wearing a coat?" asked Sabre.

"Good question," answered Ms. Croom. "Let's go and find out."

We all walked through the gates of the cemetery and were told by the people that could see that the little girl was pointing at a tombstone, smiled and then disappeared.

"Where did she go?" screamed Johnny a great kid that attends the camp every year.

"Whaaaat dooo yooou meeann?" I stammered. "She's gone? She disappeared just like that?" I asked again.

"Wow, that is really freaky," Ms. Croom stated. "Let's go and see where she was pointing."

We all walked over to the grave, Ms. Croom screamed.

"The Girl in the Blue Coat"

Ms. Croom screamed all of the other O&M's came running. Ms. Davis, Ms. Adams and Mrs. Mitchell ran over to see what was going on.

"The girl just disappeared," Ms. Croom stammered. "I looked down to where she was pointing and I saw this."

She picked up a cluster of field poppies in several beautiful colors. Ms. Croom described each one to us and let us feel of the flowers. Mrs. Mitchell then told us that the poppy flowers symbolize remembrance after a soldier died during battle.

"She was pointing to this date," Ms. Croom said. "It says that this person fought and died in the Revolutionary War in 1775."

"Wow," Josselyn said. "That is really a long time ago."

"Yes," Mr. Tommy spoke up. "This cemetery has various people and dates all throughout it. It is a very historical cemetery for veterans."

"Who cares about history," Johnny said.

"Yea," Esmeralda added.

"History class bores me to death," I moaned.

"Kids, don't you know that people in history lived and died so that you and I have and live in a safe and wonderful country," Mr. Tommy scolded. He had me on that one.

"Why do I care?" asked Ashley. "I don't know any of these people."

We were all agreeing with each other and not wanting to be lectured to by the adults.

"You kids need history lessons more than anyone since you don't appreciate it," Mr. Tommy grunted.

After our walk we went into the classroom and began working on our Braille reading.

"Oh, no," Josselyn and Kevin moaned. "We have to read about the Revolutionary War?"

"Yes, Josselyn and Kevin, you all obviously do not understand what really took place. The little girl in the coat was trying to say something to you. If she was indeed a little girl," Mrs. Glover replied.

"The American Revolution"

After I read the facts about the war and discussed it with my friends, I was a little ashamed of not being interested before. I always knew about George Washington but to be honest cutting down the cherry tree and being the first president was about it. I found out that even chopping down the cherry tree was a myth, but the other facts about him and the Revolutionary War were really incredible.

Mrs. Preston began explaining really cool facts to us as we wrote in our note taker and she called them Fast Facts. Here they are:

1. The American Revolutionary War

began in 1775 and is also known as The American Revolution.

2. British soldier and American patriots started the war in Massachusetts.
3. Colonists in American wanted to be free from England and their king.
4. The British were trying to enforce taxes but the Patriots didn't want England to have control over them.
5. There was no government at the time, so George Washington who was a military officer and wealthy Virginian was appointed Commander in Chief of the Continental Congress.
6. Congress wrote a letter to the king, King George of England and made a list of their complaints and unfair treatment.
7. On July 4, 1776, Continental Congress adopted the Declaration of Independence and were free from England.
8. The war ended in 1783, and The United States was born.
9. The Boston Tea Party was when Colo-

nist wanted the tea from England taken back. Because the British governor of Boston was not going to send the tea back the Colonists threw the tea off the boat and into the Boston Harbor.

10. Betsy Ross was a flag maker who was approaches by George Washington and other members of the Continental Congress to make a flag.

After our history lesson, we were talking about The Boston Tea Party.

"Man, I would have loved that," Ernesto laughed. "I would have thrown the tea right into that British governor's face."

"I know you would have," laughed Ashley and Johnny.

"You know what's really weird?" I asked.

"What?" Johnny wanted to know.

"The little girl in the blue coat was pointing to the same time era on the tombstone that we studied today." I continued, "She was pointing to the date April 1775."

"That is weird," Ashley said.

After the program ended for that day, I talked nonstop to my mom about The Revolutionary War.

"Yes, Abby, I know," she laughed. "I love history and study it to this day," Mom beamed. "I went to George Washington's home in Virginia and took a tour. It is called Mount Vernon and is simply beautiful.

Since he was also involved in the American Revolutionary War I also know an interesting fact about President Washington's teeth.

Some people said that he had wooden teeth or dentures, however, his false teeth were really made from animal teeth."

"Gross!" I yelled. "Can we talk about him after dinner? Oh, yeah, and remind me to tell you about the ghost," I stated.

"Civil Wars"

The next day at camp we were swimming. I love to hang out with Sabre, Josselyn, Ashley, Esmeralda, and all of the other girls. I will admit that some of the boys aren't so bad either.

We were hanging out and waiting on our O&M's to come and help us out of the dressing room when we were introduced to double trouble.

"Girls, I want you to meet two sisters, twins, actually," Ms. Gray told us. "This is Malyn and her twin Meredith."

"Hi," I said to them, but there was no answer.

"I said, hi," I repeated to the girls.

"Mrs. Gray, can these two hear?" I asked.

"Girls, say hello to Abby," Mrs. Gray pushed. I heard two sounds of grunts and then I stomped off. I hate to be around anyone that is rude."

"Have you met the twins?" I asked Esmeralda.

"I tried to meet them but they were not very nice back to me," she said.

"Who needs stuck-up kids? Let's join our own club and leave them out," I spoke.

The four of my buddies and I were having a great time, talking to Ernesto, Anthony, and Johnny when I heard someone tell me to be quiet.

"Who are you talking to?" I asked the abrupt voice.

"I am talking to you. My sister, Meredith can't hear me talking to her because your voice is so loud," Ms. Thang said back to me.

I don't know what came over me. I mean I can usually get along with everyone, but not this time. I smiled, put my arm out until

I felt of Malyn's hair and dragged her under the water.

I heard the whistle blow from Mr. Tommy and I knew that I was in a heap of trouble.

"Abby," Mr. Tommy screamed. "Get out of the pool, dry off, change your clothes and sit on the bench. I am very disappointed in you."

"Okay," I humbly replied. I loved Mr. Tommy and didn't want to make him mad at me, so I apologized to Malyn and walked into the dressing room with Ms. Croom.

"Abby, what's wrong with you?" she asked.

"I can't stand those two new girls," I said. "They are hateful, rude and just plain mean," I snorted.

"Abby," Ms. Croom said softly, "Please try to get along with them. Neither one has very much sight."

"Well, I can't see the nose on my own face, but I don't act like a creep," I snorted again.

"Yes, that's true, but did you get taken away from your parents because they were beating you so badly?" Ms. Croom snorted.

Ooops. I hate when adults do that to you. They allow you to say all kind of mean things and then they lower the boom on you by saying something that makes you feel like a creep.

"I didn't know that, Ms. Croom, but that Malyn is really mean."

"I know she is Abby and she is very protective of her sister because she has had to be the strong one for all eleven years of her life. She's never been a kid. I'll work on her attitude and you work on yours, deal?" I agreed, sat on the cold wet bench in my shorts and t-shirt whenever I heard a body sit down next to me.

"I'm sorry, Abby," mumbled a small voice belonging to the evil twin.

"It's okay. I'm sorry, too." We both sat there and didn't say another word. I mean what else could we have said? That we were now members of Ya-Ya Sisterhood or something like that?

When it was time to get back on the bus, I heard the kids screaming, "Hurry, get on the bus," they yelled.

"Why?" I screamed.

Johnny was out of breath and said, "It's the ghost girl. I just saw her in her blue coat. She's walking around the pool."

As we got on the bus I heard Mrs. Preston laughing really hard and then Ms. Kelli spoke up,

"Guys, you don't really believe that the little girl is a ghost, do you?"

No one replied. We just sat in silence while the adults laughed their heads off.

Ms. Debbie helped me off of the bus, and we were now ready for another history lesson although today I was a little more excited.

"Bubble Headed Bleach Blonde"

The following Monday, we broke into groups and wrote a newscast about the Revolutionary War. It was cool. We made up a current day newscast but discussed the war like it was happening now. I was the news anchor, Josselyn was the weather girl, Johnny was the sports announcer and Fernanda was the other news anchor.

This was my speech, "Good morning, Dallas. As you know America is getting really tired of the king and his crazy taxes, so today several of our colonists threw tea into the Boston Harbor. The English governor was furious. Watch the clip of him yelling and stomping his feet as the tea is being tossed into the ocean. More in a few minutes. Now to you, Josselyn, how's the weather?"

Josselyn spoke, "Well, hello Abby, the weather is going to be hot and sunny. The British Army will have trouble wearing those hot old hats and thick red coats all day today while the colonists who are clothed in lighter coolers should be a little more comfortable than their enemies. Now for our sports news, heeeerreeee'ssss Johnny," she barked.

"Hello. Wow! We have all kind of running going on today. Watch my clip of the British army running. Look at the dark haired man. He can really run fast."

We were laughing so hard that we could barely do our presentation.

After a fun day of being an anchor person, swimming and getting into trouble, I dropped down on my bed and took a three hour nap.

"The Girl in the Blue Coat"

The next day when we went on our walk, Malyn and Meredith walked beside my gang and me. They really weren't bad kids when you got to know them and knew why they acted as they did.

"Oh, my gosh!" I heard Ms. Kelli scream.

"What's going on?" I asked.

"Abby, up ahead we see the girl in the blue coat again, but this time she is wearing a hood that is slightly covering her face." Johnny stammered.

"Isn't it too hot to be wearing a coat?" I asked.

"Not to her. She even looks a little blue in the face," Johnny stated.

We stopped walking and waited to see what the girl was going to do next.

According to Ashley she was wandering around the tombstones, paused at one and nodded her head as if to say 'yes'. She then pointed down at one of the tombstones and disappeared again.

"The North Verses the South"

I heard Ashley scream really loud and then heard Johnny hugging and calming her down.

"Abby, the little girl just disappeared again," Johnny said in a stunned tone.

"We need to find out what is written on that tombstone," I said.

"Yes, and that's exactly where we are going now," Johnny asked.

"Now?" I squeaked. "Are you completely nuts?" I yelled again.

"Abby, it's okay. She's not there anymore," Ernesto said softly.

"I bet she is," I screamed. "I will walk over to the grave and she'll pull me down under the ground and I'll never see my family again." I had worked myself up so much that my heart began palpitating.

"Okay, fine, Abby, you wait here, while the rest of us go and find out," Johnny said.

"You're not leaving me here," I squalled.

"Make up your mind," Ernesto screamed. "Women drive me crazy," he said.

"Okay, I'll go but only if I stay by you, Ernesto," I said.

So off we went to the grave and probably face-to-face with a dead kid.

"Wow," Johnny said. "The tombstone says that this person, John Chambers, fought against his own brother during the Civil War. He fought for the south and his brother was fighting for the north."

"I know about The Revolutionary War. So tell me about the Civil War?" I asked.

"Abby, don't you ever pay attention in class?" laughed Johnny. "I love history so that class keeps me wide awake," Johnny continued.

We sat down on the grass once we got back to the school and listened while Johnny gave us some cool facts about The Civil War.

1. The Civil War lasted from 1861 to 1865
2. The southern states wanted their own laws but the north did not want the United States to be broken apart
3. In 1860, Abraham Lincoln ran for office and wanted to end slavery. The south said that if Lincoln was elected then they would break apart from the north and become their own nation and were called The Confederate States of American.
4. President Lincoln was forced to declare war in order to end slavery
5. The war was long and bloody
6. The south was defeated by the north
7. General Lee was the leader over the Confederacy and General Grant was the leader over the war
8. Lee surrendered to Grant at Appomattox Court House in Virginia

9. The war was over
10. Our nation was never divided again

"Life is But a Dream"

I was sitting near the back of the group while Johnny gave us these incredible facts about The Civil War.

I was really taking in the knowledge when I heard a whisper in my ear.

"Aaaabbbbyyyyy. Aaaaaabbbbbbyyyyyyy. Did you enjoy your life?" The voice whispered and then sang,

"Life is but a dream" from the famed "Row, Row Row Your Boat".

Oh, my gosh! It was the girl in the blue coat again.

"Heeeeeelp me," I begged the group, but no one seemed to hear me.

I was then petrified so I yelled as loud as I could "Somebody please help me."

The voice whispered to me, "I'll help you. Follow me to the grave. I want you to stay there with me. I have a nice red coat like the British wore in the Revolutionary War if you like."

"Nooooooooooo!!!" I screamed like a mad woman. The next thing I felt was my mother waking me up. I was having another one of my famous nightmares. I guess I went to sleep later that afternoon and was dreaming about what Johnny told us earlier in the day.

"Abby did you eat onions tonight or is this silly talk about a ghost getting to you?" she asked.

"Mom, our Summer Skills Program group keeps seeing a girl ghost and she keeps pointing to old tombstones. The person under all of that dirt was somehow involved in one of the wars," I choked.

"Well, at least she's a patriotic ghost," Mom joked.

"This isn't funny," I said.

"Abby, there is a logical explanation for this. Ghosts just don't go around pointing at tombstones and scaring kids," Mom said.

The rest of the night I was a wreck. My dang wristwatch kept crowing, "2am, 3am, 4am, etc, etc, etc

"Bowling Fun"

The next day was so much fun even though I was incredibly drowsy from not sleeping the night before.

"Everybody line up," said Ms. Debbie.

We all lined up and hung out together on the bus.

"Hey, Abby. Can we sit here by you?" asked Malyn.

"Sure Malyn. There's room for everyone."

I get mad when my feelings are hurt easily, but I also get over my feelings pretty quickly, too.

Mr. Tommy and the teachers lined us up and put us into partners for bowling. Even though I don't like to admit it, I needed the bowling pads.

"Knock them down!" Ernesto yelled. "Strike, Abby!" he screamed.

Everybody was cheering really loud for me and I was cheering really loud for everyone else. Sometimes having a visual impairment has its advantages.

After bowling we headed towards the school.

"Okay, let's get off the bus and go inside where it is nice and cool," Mr. Tommy said.

We were all laughing and climbing down off of the bus when I heard a big hush.

"What's going on?" I asked.

"Abby, I hate to be the one to tell you, but the girl in the blue coat is back at it again," moaned Ashley.

"The Girl in the Blue Coat"

According to Joseph the girl was not covered up by the hood this time and he could see her nodding her head slowly and pointing again and 'poof' she was gone.

"Well at least she didn't want company this time," I joked but scared at the same time.

"Esmeralda, run over there and see what she's pointing to now," I said.

"No, thank you," Esmeralda said and continued,

"Dead girls and I do not get along."

"I'll go," Malyn said. So Malyn, Ernesto and Joseph went over to the cemetery.

"No surprise, here," Joseph said.

"She was pointing to a time in our history that was a very tough era for everyone.

This war was World War II and there are many sad facts about this time period," Ernesto said honestly.

Ernesto began telling us facts about World War II .

1. In 1918, Germany lost World War 1. It was banned from having armed forces
2. In 1933 the German people voted for a leader named Adolf Hitler who was a Nazis
3. Hitler promised to make his country strong again
4. Germany attacked Poland, so Britain and France declared war on Germany
5. Under Hitler's guidance the Nazis sought to make Germany the most powerful country
6. Hitler was full of hate and killed many innocent Jewish people and others who were not German
7. The United States joined the battle

when Pearl Harbor was bombed by the Japanese. The Japanese had sided with Germany.

8. The war ended and Hitler was defeated

When we were back in the classroom, Ms. Glover and Mrs. Davis began teaching us all about World War II.

"That Hitler guy was nuts," Ashley said.

"He sure was," I agreed. "I feel so sad for so many people who lived during this time. I'm going home to talk to my Nana about this," I told the group.

Nana gave me even more facts about this era because she was born in the late 30's right before this sad time in world history.

"Abby, I don't remember much because I was so young, but I can remember the stories that my mother and dad told me," Nan remembered.

"Our country was in a great depression. Many people lost their jobs and money during the time from 1929-1940. President

Roosevelt was elected into office from 1933 to 1945. He started programs that really helped our country. He's also famous for a quote, "You have nothing to fear but fear itself."

"Wow, thanks, Nana. I didn't realize how interesting history really is. I'll call you this weekend and let's go shop 'til we drop."

I laughed, hung up the phone and went to bed.

"The Girl in the Blue Coat"

The last day of Summer Skills Program was really sad for all of us. We had formed so many tight friendships with other kids who dealt with having a vision problem and other kid issues. We really got close after we discussed dating, friends, technology for the blind and many other issues that only people who have a visual impairment can understand.

We were sitting on the bleachers and eating snacks in the gym whenever I heard the some of the kids begin to yell.

"What is it?" I yelled.

"Itttt'sssss the giiirrrrlllllll ghost," screamed both Kevin Johnny.

To our surprise, the adults began laughing and cutting up with each other.

"What is it?" I begged.

"It's Ms. Julie wearing a blue coat," Ashley laughed. Oh, my gosh. The girl ghost that we were all frightened of was in fact Ms. Julie.

"Why were you doing that to us?" we all asked.

"Because all you ever did was talk about how boring history was. We all wanted you to see how exciting it really is and how it affects our freedom today."

Whew! I was so relieved until Kevin asked a question.

"Mrs. Julie, where is the hood on your blue coat? We saw it on your coat the day that your face looked really blue." he said.

"What hood?" Mrs. Julie asked. "My coat never had a hood."

THE END

Abby Diamond's "Secrets in the Attic"

BY: Kristie Smith-Armand M.Ed

"One of the **secrets** of life is that all that is really worth the doing is what we do for others" Lewis Carroll

"Introduction"

This summer was turning into one of the most exciting summers of my life.

After I attended Vision Skills Camp for the Blind and Visually Impaired after real school was out I was afraid that I was going to be bored. Boy was I wrong.

While spending time at summer camp we learned about three famous wars: The American Revolutionary War, the Civil War and World War II, oh yeah, and we met a ghost but you probably already knew all of that.

The next Monday after I received awards for all of my hard work at Vision Skills Camp,

I called Neils, Andrea and Alison to come over and hang out with me.

"Hey, Abby, I'll be right over," Andrea squealed as did Neils and Alison. When they walked into the room, Neils began at once,

"Man, I was so glad that you called," she said. "My older brothers are really getting on my nerves, big time!" Neils barked.

"I'm so glad y'all came, too. I mean after the camp I have to entertain Chip all day. I love the little guy, but geez, I need a break."

"Abby," Mom called.

"Yep," I yelled back. I guess this was going to be too much yelling, so she walked into my room and said,

"Would you and the girls mind going up to the attic and bringing me my old school year books? I'm going to my twenty-five year high school reunion and I wanted to display them on our 'meet and greet' table."

"Wow, Mrs. Diamond," Neils chirped. "You don't look nearly that old. Wow, you don't even have that many wrinkles." Even though my eyes don't see I can still roll them.

My mother muttered a 'thank you, I think' under her breath and left out of the room.

"Neils, you are something else," Andrea laughed. Alison laughed too and said,

"Neils, do not ever say those words to my mother, Kaitlyn. She will never speak to you or me again."

We died laughing. I mean Kaitlyn is an awesome movie star, so it was only appropriate that Neils be fair-warned.

"Okay, Guys. I have to ask a dumb question," I said.

"Go ahead and ask," Neils encouraged.

"I don't know what or where my attic is."

"Oh man Abby, I bet you don't. Unless you had a reason to go to the attic, how would you know?"

I was led up a flight of stairs from which I did know existed.

"Man, these stairs creak," I said.

"Your house is old, Abby. It's beautiful and swanky but it is old," Andrea told me.

"Yea, I know. Our houses in this neighborhood are very expensive but they are old and historical.

My mother once told me that the house belonged to Grandmother Elizabeth when she was a child," I said.

We walked up the creaky staircase and into the smelly old musky attic. My buddies began to look for the year books from Mom's good 'ol glory days.

"I found them," Andrea called out.

I could hear pages turning from a book when Alison said,

"Abby, your mom looked just like you when she was in high school. I mean just like you."

I could hear Andrea and Alison chatting away about the early eighties and the funky styles when we heard a loud creak and Neils scream, "Oh, my gosh!"

"The Secret Door"

"Neils, what is it?" I screamed. I banged my head on something hard and then got caught in a spider web. Needless to say, I went crazy. "Help me!" I yelled.

To my relief, I heard Neils laughing so hard.

"Here, Abby let me help you," Neils chuckled.

"Why did you scream?" I asked.

"There is the coolest secret door right here in the attic, so I gently opened it up and guess what, Guys? You are never going to believe what I saw inside.

"Is it a body without a head?" Alison said in a really shaky voice.

"Hahahahha," Neils laughed. "You crack me up, Alison." Neils continued, "Let's all go inside. Look at this cool and hidden room, and, Abby, you are not going to believe this." We walked inside the small musky-smelling room and I heard a familiar 'tap, tap, tap' sound.

"Neils, that sounds kinda like a Braille writer," I said.

"Give the lady a rose," Neils teased.

"Give me a rose?" I questioned.

Neils laughed and explained, "If you say to give the lady a rose it is someone being sarcastic. In other words what you just said could have gone without saying.

Andrea changed the subject and said,

"Abby, this is very old Braille writer."

She led me to the Braille writer while I placed my hands on the keys.

"Oh, my gosh, y'all. Look, this key makes dot 1, this one makes dot 2, while the others make their own dots, 3, 4, 5, and 6. In Braille there are six dots in a Braille cell. Dots 1, 2 and 3 are on the left side of the cell and dots 4, 5, and 6 are on the right. Now the question of the day, Folks, who does this Braille writer belong to and what is it doing in my attic?"

"Selma"

"Abby, look over here," Alison screamed.

"Hey, Alison I would love to but I can't," I teased.

"Oh, Abby, come toward my voice. It looks like a very old Braille book. Oh, my gosh, there are more Braille books in this box," Alison said.

I placed my hands all over the old dusty books. Man, was I excited. The pages felt and smelled really old.

"What type of books are they?" asked Andrea. "

"Well, this one appears to be a reader with some guy named Ned and this one is an old English book. Yuck, in the olden days they also had to suffer through the parts of speech," I laughed.

We were laughing and having a blast when I found a true treasure and one that would once again change my life.

"Selma's Diary"

"Guys," I said, "This is someone's diary. Her name was Selma. It says right here that she was born in 1892. She also says that she finally received a Braille writer at the age of eight years."

"Read more," Neils, always the adventurous one screamed.

"Okay, Neils. Guys, do y'all really want to hear this?"

I didn't have to ask twice because my best buddies were soon gathered around me breathless. We were reading and finding out about Selma's life. Selma was like me and was born without any sight, so she, like me, didn't know what it was like to see. Selma was still single and complaining because she was already twenty and considered an old maid.

"What's an old maid?" Neils questioned.

"You met my aunt Dana, right?"

"Yep," Neils responded.

"Well, by old standards a woman who was not married by age twenty, wore old lady clothes and never had dates with men were considered Old Maids. Remember the card game when no one wanted to draw the 'Old Maid' card?" "However," I continued. "Selma was no old maid. She had dates and was considered beautiful by most people."

Selma was the only child of two hard-working but honest people named Dale and Liza. Even though Dale and Liza didn't have much money they were determined to send Selma away to school so that she could learn how to read and write in Braille.

Luckily during the early part of the century Texas School for the Blind existed and far better than what Louis Braille had experienced in Paris.

Back in the 1800's according to Selma's diary, Louis Braille and other children who were blind were not allowed to read or write in the code even after Louis Braille's invention. They were mistreated and often abused at a school in Paris.

Many times the children who were visually impaired were locked up for hours in rooms without food.

When Selma went to Texas School for the Blind in the early 1900's children were taught life skills and academics. According to the diary, Selma and the other girls who were visually impaired were taught to sew, basket weave, bead work, piano tuning, mattress making and broom making. They made their own clothes and shoes and sold brooms door-to-door for the school while the guys worked on the horse and buggy carriages, learned mechanics and other industrial skills.

My friends and I were all caught up in Selma's story whenever we heard Chip call,

"AAAbbbby, Mommy wants you."

"Okay, I am coming," I yelled back. "Come on Guys, let's hurry downstairs. I don't want anyone else to know about this room," I said.

We did our secret friendship shake, jumped out of the room and raced down the staircase.

The next morning I had planned to sleep in but that did not happen when my cell phone began buzzing.

"Hey Abby are you still asleep?" questioned Neils. "What gave me away?" I mumbled. "The slurred speech or the fact that it is 7 o'clock am," I joked.

"Get up, Abby. I have already called Andrea and Alison. Girl, we cannot wait to hear more of Selma's diary."

"Great," I said. "Mom has taken Chip to a play group in the neighborhood and then they're going over to Harry and Grandmother Elizabeth's house all afternoon. We have the house to ourselves."

Around 10:00 everyone arrived and up the staircase we went.

"Rich Man, Poor Man"

"Abby, I can't wait to hear what Selma is up to today," Alison stated.

"Well, let's get comfortable and see what happened next in her life," I said. Right after I spoke the four of us heard a loud clap of thunder, and we screamed.

"WOW!" Neils yelped. "Let's sit closer together and listen."

The rain was pouring hard on the roof, and it was really loud.

We gathered several old blankets from an old trunk and made beds across the floor.

We huddled together and got ready for the next 'Selma adventure!'

I continued reading and we were amazed.

Selma left the school for the blind when she was nineteen. Although she was very happy at the school she was excited to leave and live on her own.

Selma became very fluent in Braille reading and writing and began to work in a factory.

She wrote, "Since the war started, I am finally allowed to work in the factory. I hate this job, but it is a job that is paying fairly well. I am going to save up my money and travel to a faraway place."

According to the diary, Selma traveled. While she hated the factory, she met many great friends who were around her age. One friend, that she was particularly fond of was a young woman named Marilyn, Mare for short. Mare was from England, and immediately took to Selma. They became fast friends, ate lunch together daily, and at times with their other girl friends, and would go out at night on the town.

Mare eventually moved back to England, but the two young women stayed friends and kept in frequent contact by mailing each other weekly.

One day Selma got the most wonderful news- Mare was getting married, and she wanted Selma to be her maid-of-honor. Selma was so excited to go to England but could not afford to travel.

However, Mare was marrying a wealthy man and paid her way to England on a ship named, 'The Alfred.'

Selma writes, "I have never been one for motion and am easily motion sick, but the ship is enormous, and I am having a wonderful time and meeting all types of people on my way to England. This is an adventure that I would have hated to miss." I stopped reading for a minute because my fingers were tired.

"Keep going, Abby," Andrea said. "I have got to hear about this wedding."

"I will, I promise, but let's go downstairs and eat lunch. We still have several hours before Chip and Mom will be back." We went downstairs and made bologna and cheese sandwiches with salty potato chips. I cracked open a large tub of ice cream and opened up the soda.

"This Selma lady is so interesting," Andrea commented.

"I know," I said. "I am impressed with her having no sight and traveling on a large ship by herself to England to see Mare."

"That is so cool about the horse and buggies," Alison said. "I didn't even think about the fact that there were few automobiles around that time."

Neils was crunching like there was no tomorrow. Crunch, crunch, crunch, and then began talking with her mouth full.

"Neils, wait until you are finished eating before you start talking," I scolded.

"How did you know I was eating with my mouth full?" Neils questioned.

"Because," I continued. "You sound like 'mmmmmffffmmff'." We all laughed, ate and finished our lunch with spoons and a tub of ice cream.

"Okay," Alison said. "Abby let's go back upstairs and see what Selma is up to now."

We climbed back up the staircase and went into the secret room.

Selma made it to England and Mare was waiting at the dock for her.

Selma found out quickly that Mare was not the happy-go-lucky young woman that she once had been. It seemed that Mare's rich young husband was not rich or very nice but wanted her to marry him anyway.

He was so persistent and Mare was frightened of him.

Neils spoke up and interrupted,

"I wouldn't take that from nobody," she announced.

"Take that from NOBODY?" Andrea asked. "Neils, how many times do I have to tell you to stop speaking like Jaxson. You can hang out with him, but stop speaking like him. You should have said, 'I would not take that from ANYONE.'"

We all died laughing, and then I continued.

Mare begged Selma to help her escape, so the two girls quickly planned a really quick exit. They pulled their money together, and as luck would have it bought their tickets on a maiden voyage called the Titanic. Neils, Andrea, Alison and I all screamed in unison,

"The Titanic!"

We then heard a loud clap of thunder, hard rain pouring, and the lights went out.

"The Unsinkable Ship"

Selma said that the ship was considered the most elaborate ship that had ever been built. It was so large that it was like a floating city and was unsinkable.

Selma and Mare felt so lucky to have purchased tickets on this floating paradise. However, because the girls lacked for money, they had to purchase third class passenger tickets.

Neither Selma nor Mare wanted to be stationed in the bowels of the boat, but what choice did they have?

Neils spoke up and interrupted again, "Bowels of the boat, gross!"

"Neils, be quieted," we all screamed.

"Soooorrry," she moped.

At first, Selma and Mare really enjoyed the luxury ship. It was equipped with a swimming pool, a gym, two libraries and a Turkish bath. Mare took Selma all over the ship and the two began meeting people from France, Iran, England and the United States. Selma writes that this was truly the "time of her life." For four days the girls laughed, ate, danced and met many more wonderful people until the night of April 14th, not long before midnight. Mare and Selma were out on the deck talking to two friends John and Sammy when there was a huge bump. Selma fell down and felt a large piece of ice on the deck. She wrote,

"I asked myself, 'What is a large piece of ice was doing on the deck'?"

Pretty soon she heard the terrible news; the Titanic ship hit an ice burg and the unsinkable ship was going to sink."

The four of us were taking all of this history in when we heard a car door slam.

"Your mom and Chip are back, Abby!" Andrea said.

"Let's get out of here and pick up later," Alison echoed.

We ran down the stairs and plopped on the couch like we had been sitting there for days.

"Sinking"

"You girls are awfully calm," Mom teased.

"How's the reunion planning going?" asked Neils. As glad as I was that she helped my mom to change the subject, I was hoping Neils wasn't going to talk about her wrinkles again.

"It is going great Neils, I bought more wrinkle cream yesterday." she laughed. Neils cracked up laughing, too. The rest of the day we sat around and watched television.

"No offense, Abby, but I wish your parents were leaving tonight, so that we could hear more about Selma and Mare," Alison said.

"Guys, I have an idea," I said. "Wait right here."

I came back and announced,

"Guess what? We have tomorrow afternoon and night all to ourselves. I talked to Katy, and she said that she wants Chip to come over and play with Brennan. Mom and Dad are going to the reunion."

"How did you arrange that?" Andrea asked.

"Well, I heard Mom say that they were going to the reunion, so I made a quick call to Katy and sort of invited Chip to their house. Katy said that she wanted to see Chip any way." We were excited about the night all ahead, just Selma and us.

I could hear Mom the next day making a hair appointment, ironing her dress and getting ready for her big reunion. She sounded so excited. Dad was less enthusiastic.

"Abby, I cannot wait to see some of my best friends who moved away years ago. We are going to have the most wonderful time!"

"Mom, have a great time and don't worry about me because the gang is coming over tonight to stay with me. Is it okay if they all spend the night?" I asked.

"Why sure, Abby," Mom answered. "The gang is always welcomed in my home." Finally my parents and Chippy left and the gang was here with me.

We were laughing and giggling acting like the preadolescents that we were, when we raced up the staircase toward the secrets in the attic.

"Abby, over here is a trunk full of items," Andrea said.

I walked over to the trunk and inside it were strange objects like a bowl, a crystal glass, an old hairbrush, a dress, a hat and a pair of crazy-feeling stockings.

"What in the heck?" I questioned and continued,

"Why would you have a few odds and ends in a trunk for safe-keeping?"

"Great question, Abby. Maybe the answer lies in the journal. Girl, get to reading," Andrea barked.

We laughed, so I picked up the diary and began reading.

Selma said that the air was unbelievably cold. Sammy and John huddled around her and Mare and took them inside of the big sinking ship.

"It all my fault," said a man's voice.

"Who is that?" Mare asked.

"It is Thomas Andrews." John answered. "He is the designer of the ship. I guess he is blaming himself for the sinking of the Titanic."

Selma said that what happened next was total chaos. People were running and screaming and trying to get on a lifeboat. The bigger problem facing the doomed ship was that there weren't enough lifeboats for all of the passengers aboard the ship. The final verdict was that women and children would be first, and of course, the first class passengers would be the ones to get off the sinking ship.

Sammy screamed,

"Let's get these girls on a boat."

Selma begged Sammy and John to stay with her and Mare when all of a sudden the big ship began to break apart.

There were screams and loud shouting, when all of a sudden somebody grabbed Selma and put her on a lifeboat without Mare, Sammy or John.

Selma wrote,"I had never been so scared in all my life. Someone grabbed my arm and said that I should get on board immediately. I yelled and yelled for Mare but the screams were drowning out my voice. I could feel the small lifeboat sailing away from the sounds of screams and chaos.

I met a wonderful lady named Molly Brown who was from Colorado. She took my arm and consoled me,

"Don't you worry, Honey. Everything will be alright."

Nonetheless, Selma was worried sick about Mare.

The Carpathia picked up the survivors from the life boats and took them home. The crew took great care of the survivors from the sinking ship.

"That's terrible." Neils moaned.

"I know," Andrea echoed.

"I am dying to find out what happened to Mare," I said, so I continued to read.

Selma walked the boat crying and upset.

She was so worried about Mare and her new friends, Sammy and John when she heard a familiar voice,

"Selma, I'm okay."

It was Mare. Selma said that the two grabbed each other and hugged.

"Let me introduce you to someone who saved me. This is Jesse."

Mare told Selma that Jesse, and a sweet girl named Maime grabbed her and put her on the lifeboat.

It would be the last boat and the last seat to be taken.

Selma said, "Mare was touched by a wonderful woman named Maude who took her to the life boats, but who herself was not saved."

"What about Sammy and John?" asked Alison.

"I'm getting there." I said.

By the time the boat sailed to New York, word had spread that the great unsinkable ship, had in fact, sank killing many of her passengers that she vowed to protect.

Selma and Mare got off the ship arm-in-arm. They heard two voices shouting. "Girls, wait up!" It was Sammy and John. The two had miraculously been awarded seats on the lifeboats.

This was surprising because the men only made up twenty percent of the survivors.

Neils, Andrea, Alison and I all cheered whenever I read that the men were also saved.

"Keep reading," Andrea begged.

Selma vowed after the disaster aboard the ship to keep the items from the Titanic, always. The bowl and the glass were gifts from the Titanic ship makers. Selma had also carefully taken off the clothes she wore that fateful night and stored them for safe keeping. It was her way of memorializing the journey of the sinking of the mighty ship.

"Oh!!" Neils screamed. "The items in the trunk are actually from the Titanic. I can't believe this."

I couldn't believe it either. I was stunned.

"I wonder what happened to the four of them. Maybe we'll find out if we keep reading," Alison said.

Mare ended up marrying a lawyer from New York and had three wonderful children, two girls and one boy. Sammy was a prominent lawyer who married a beautiful woman named Mare.

"Oh, my gosh!" we all screamed.

John and the rest of the group stayed in close contact. Although John never married he was a very noteworthy professor and lived a long good life. And Selma... Selma became a successful author and married a wealthy businessman and gave birth to Melissa. I closed the book and was speechless as was the rest of the gang because we realized that Selma had to be somehow related to me.

"Am I kin to Selma?" We all screamed and they begged me to read more.

"Another Mystery"

Molly Brown had been the woman to save Selma on that fateful night aboard the Titanic. Molly's husband, Johnny was once a gold miner and then advanced to superintendent of the mine. A superintendent of a mine was a promotion but not like the one that he was about to obtain. He invented a device that gets the gold out of the bottom of the mine making him and Molly very rich.

Molly and "Leadville Johnny" were two very wealthy people who continued to help others with their money. They helped build a Roman Catholic Church, ran soup kitchens for the poor and were philanthropist throughout their lives.

"What a philanthropist?" asked Neils.

"They are rich people who give away their money for great causes that help others."

"I give Jaxson money for ice cream every week," Neils added. "Am I a philanthropist?"

Andrea chuckled, "Sort of, but you don't have millions to give away."

I continued...

I stopped when I was once again interrupted by Neils.

"Two more questions, and then I will be quiet," Neils said.

"No you won't," I added, "But go ahead and ask."

"Why was Molly's husband called 'Leadville Johnny' and what in the heck is a soup kitchen?" Neils pondered.

"Okay," I began using my 'teacher' voice. "To answer your first question, 'Leadville Johnny' was Johnny's nickname because he was responsible for getting to the bottom of the gold mines through his invention that was able to grab any ounce of gold left in the mine. You also asked what a soup kitchen was.

During the Great Depression when our country was poor people had to stand in soup lines to get fed. Some of the people who stood in the lines for soup were once wealthy people, but during this time they lost all of their money. Now can I get back to Molly and Selma?" I asked. After Neils grunted a yes, I continued.

Molly headed the Denver's Women's Club and worked in the juvenile courts.

She and Selma kept in contact through writing letters weekly and they became close friends.

One night Molly and Johnny were throwing a huge party, so they invited Selma to come to Denver and attend. They would pay all costs if Selma would join them. Selma talked it over with her parents, Dale and Liza who were encouraging her to go and have some fun like other girls her age. The night of the party was everything Selma thought it would be and more.

She was hob-knobbing with the rich and famous. One man in particular named Benjamin asked her to dance. They not only danced but only talked to each other for the rest of the night. Ben started sending letters to Selma daily and she returned each one.

Within a year the two had a beautiful wedding in Denver at the home of Molly Brown.

"Oh, Abby. Come over here and look at this wedding gown. It has to be Selma's," Neils said.

We all ran over to the large trunk that held the Titanic items and sure enough there was an elegant long laced wedding dress. The sleeves were covered in lace.

"WOW," Andrea said. "Even though the dress is ancient and smells musky it is still one of the most beautiful dresses ever."

"How did you find it, Neils?" I asked.

"Well, I was listening to the story and wondered what else might be in the trunk.

I found a box with stuffed with packing and found the dress tucked tightly inside."

Alison continued to dig inside of the trunk and found a delicate blue garter belt and beside it was a tiny pink gown.

"Abby, feel of the garter belt. My mom told me that it is tradition in our family and many others for the bride to wear a garter around your thigh and under the wedding dress. After the ceremony the groom takes off the garter belt and throws it towards a group of single men who fight to get it."

"Abby, can we take a food and bathroom break?" asked Neils.

"Sure, we can come back to the diary later," I said simply.

"No," they all screamed.

"Short bathroom and food break," barked Alison. "Yes Sir," Neils yelled and laughed.

We ran downstairs took a quick break and ran back up into the attic to find out about the baby and the pink gown. After the beautiful and lavish wedding, Selma, Ben, Liza and Dale all moved into a beautiful mansion in Dallas, Texas. Within the year, Selma found out that she was going to have a baby. Everything seemed perfect. Liza and Selma sewed clothes for the new family member while Dale and Ben painted one of the rooms and made the most gorgeous nursery for the baby. Selma was very sick throughout the next nine months and sat in the house for hours on end.

She began writing children's stories to take her mind off of the extreme discomfort that woke her up every morning and never left throughout the day in order to ensure the health of the baby and a safe arrival.

Selma and Ben were elated when she gave birth to a baby girl named. . .

"Named what?" Neils screamed. "And nobody better yell at me this time."

"Guys, the next page is missing," I said distraughtly.

"What?" The mob was growing angry.

"Wait a minute. Here's the next page," I said. They let out a sigh of relief.

I read the next line silently with my hands and screamed out, "I knew it!"

"The Roaring 20's"

Selma gave birth to a beautiful and healthy little girl named Melissa.

"Abby is that your great grandmother?" Andrea asked.

"Yes, I believe that was my Grandmother Elizabeth's mother. Oh, my gosh! Let's read on," I said.

World War I had ended and the roaring twenties were about to begin.

"Abby. I remember hearing my grandmother telling me about jazz music and flappers from the twenties. You see, World War I had ended and the twenties were a time for the jazz era. Women rights were noticed as the women cut their hair, voted and were more assertive. For the first time, women danced in public with men. They were known as the flappers. My grandmother told me that her mother was a flapper and could really dance," Andrea said.

Just about that time Nosey Neils shouted,

"Check out this dress and hat!" Sure enough in Selma's trunk was an old flapper dress and hat.

Neils put on the dress and the hat and began dancing around. Alison looked further inside the large trunk and found an old record player and jazz album.

Andrea turned on the old player and surprisingly it still worked.

"Turn it up." Neils said.

We dug through the old trunk and found three more of Selma's dresses.

We danced, sang and were having the time of our lives when the lights went out and Neils screamed.

"What happened to the lights?" Neils asked in a calmer voice.

"It's the thunder and lightning again." Andrea said. "Abby, we don't have any light," Alison added.

"No worries for me. Sit back and relax and let me continue to read.

"1930's"

Selma and Ben were so proud of Melissa.

Selma writes, "Melissa is the best thing that has ever happened to me. She amazes me every day."

Melissa goes on to become an excellent student with a sharp tongue. Selma writes it off as a "lawyer in the making" who is interested in a military career.

After all, Selma explains, a good lawyer needs to be able to argue and Melissa was an expert in debating issues. It was the year 1929 and the economy was looking bad in the United States.

Wealthy people were losing their jobs and were being fed by soup kitchens. Selma,

Melissa and Ben while not homeless were struggling to make ends meet, so Selma began teaching writing classes at the local school, so that they would not lose their home.

Selma said, "I see people who were once wealthy now begging for work and food on the streets.

Ben and I have three families living with us until they can get jobs. It is hard on Melissa but she is helping out and keeping a great attitude."

"I know what this time period is called," Alison said. "It was the time period of the Great Depression."

I continued to read.

Finally, the United States got relief when President Roosevelt took office. He said in his infamous speech, "You have nothing to fear but fear itself." He started programs that were helping the unemployed, and it was working. After the bombing of Pearl Harbor by the Japanese, President Roosevelt called the United States into the war to help defeat the most evil man of all time Germany's Adolf Hitler.

"I am so frightened because Melissa has joined the military and is training to become a nurse.

She will be stationed in Hawaii. Melissa is too stubborn for me to try to talk her out of it."

"Poor Selma!" Andrea cried.

"Hey Guys look at this," Alison said.

Inside the large trunk was a pillow from Hawaii that said, 'Aloha means hello, Aloha means goodbye, too, but the most important thing Aloha means is I love you.'

"I bet that's from Melissa," I stated.

"Abby read on," Neils begged. "Does Melissa make it back alive? What happens to Selma? Keep reading, Girl."

I kept feeling for more Braille. I frantically turned the rest of the pages from the diary but there was nothing.

"Guys." I said slowly. "I hate to break this to you, but Selma stopped writing in her diary." We were speechless.

"Happy Birthday, Elizabeth"

After our depression lifted we walked back down the staircase and into my room.

"Man, Abby," Neils began, "I feel like I just bit into the best piece of chocolate cake and then someone jerks it out of my mouth."

I knew exactly how she felt. We decided to watch a movie and turn our thoughts elsewhere when I came up with a great idea.

"Hey, Guys, why don't we ask Elizabeth about Selma? Harry is giving her a huge birthday party, and you're all invited." I said.

"Great idea," Andrea replied.

"How old is she going to be?" Neils asked.

"Neils, I don't know but don't ask her and don't tell her how young she looks in spite of her wrinkles."

We laughed and then planned a fun day of swimming in my pool the following day.

The next morning we were swimming and having a great time. The cool swimming pool water felt so good on my skin in the 101 degree heat in the hot Texas sun.

"Neils, apply your sunscreen," my mom called out to Neils.

"Thanks Mrs. D. Hey how was your reunion last night?" she asked.

"Great and guess what, Neils? Not one person commented on my wrinkles."

We laughed, swam and ate all afternoon.

The night of the party was an exciting night.

I bought the cutest short turquoise dress with sparkled sandals.

Neils, Andrea and Alison came over and my parents, the gang and I left together for

Grandmother's Elizabeth's birthday party. When we arrived to the party there were balloons, lights, huge fountains, one being a chocolate one for kids, and all kinds of beautiful sights.

Andrea walked with me and described everything to me.

"Abby this place is simply amazing," Andrea commented.

There were scores of people there that night, also. The four of us were gathered around talking to my cousin, Brooklyn from California, eating chocolate like crazy when I heard Harry come up behind us.

"Hey Girls are y'all having a good time?" He asked in his normally cheerful voice.

"Yes, we are having a great time," Neils answered. "Harry can I ask you a question alone?" I asked. "Sure Abby. Let's walk over here."

So, Harry and I walked away from the crowd.

"Harry, the gang and I found a secret door in my house." I grinned and continued. "We discovered an old Braille writer and the diary of Grandmother Elizabeth's grandmother, Selma."

Harry was quiet for a few minutes but seemed like a lifetime to me.

"Abby, I knew her and she was a remarkable woman."

"Yes, she was," I said. "I hope that my grandmother won't mind that I read her diary."

"Not at all Abby, she'll be glad that she is not the only one in the family to have read it. I have read it also and the diary is so incredible but I have long forgotten about it," Harry said.

"Do you read Braille, too, Harry?" I asked.

"Yes, your grandmother taught me. She called Selma 'Big Mama'," Harry said.

I laughed at the name Big Mama.

"She wasn't big at all, but to a two year old she must have looked enormous," Harry chuckled recalling past wonderful memories.

"Well if you don't mind the gang and I would love to hear more about Selma, Ben, Liza, Dale and of course, Melissa," I said.

"Certainly I would be more than happy to share my wonderful memories of Selma and Melissa. I never knew why Selma suddenly stopped writing in her diary. You know she was a wonderful children's author and absolutely adored writing."

"I love to write, too," I said feeling a huge bond with Selma. I now knew where I got my love for writing, and also where I got my sharp tongue.

"I'll talk to your mom and see if she can bring you girls back over tomorrow. We can grill out and she'll tell you everything you want to know about the family."

Grandmother Elizabeth had the best time that night. She danced, opened presents and visited with everyone.. At the end of the night, we were all exhausted.

"Girls, Harry said that you would love to learn more about Selma. I'll take you over there tomorrow afternoon. How on earth did you find out about Selma?" Mom asked.

"We found a few items upstairs," I answered honestly but without giving out too much information.

After all, the four musketeers had a place now other than our little clubhouse where we could hide out.

"Nurse Nightingale"

The next afternoon the gang and I were sitting at Harry and Grandmother's picnic table in the back of their large home.

Since we swam the day before we skipped swimming and listened to Harry talk while he grilled us some really great hot dogs and burgers.

Grandmother Elizabeth was more thrilled to tell us all about her great grandmother, Selma and grandmother, Melissa.

"Tell us whatever you can remember," I said.

I had already filled in Harry and Grandmother Elizabeth where the diary left off.

"First things first, it gets confusing, so let me go over the family tree. Liza had Selma. Selma gave birth to Melissa and Melissa had me, Elizabeth. I'll save the best for last, Abby. I had your mother, Caroline and she had you. You see, Abby, our visual impairment seems to be inherited. You, Selma and I have our own bond. Selma lived a really long life and hopefully we will, too."

Grandmother Elizabeth continued telling us about our really cool family.

"Melissa was very strong willed. You remind me so much of her, Abby," Grandmother Elizabeth said softly.

Melissa became a nurse and went into battle to take care of the wounded soldiers. She was nicknamed, "Florence Nightingale" because of unwillingness to let anyone die. She, like Florence Nightingale, fought for better conditions for soldiers. Florence Nightingale was known as "The Lamp Lady" because she would walk around with her lamp and visit with the soldiers in order to console them. Because of Florence Nightingale's influence,

Melissa did the same. She would walk around and talk to the wounded soldiers.

She did not always save everyone, but she fought like a Trojan to save every human that came her way.

When the war was over, her dad back started a new business in Texas oil and that made the family really wealthy. They lived in your house until they passed away years later," Grandmother Elizabeth said proudly.

The fact that we were all so taken in by Selma seemed to thrill my Grandmother Elizabeth.

Harry served us delicious hot dogs and burgers while we ate chips and drank really sweet tea. Texans love our tea sweet on a hot summer day.

However, it was really getting hot, so after we ate we went inside where the air was blowing cool.

"Tell us more about our girl, Selma," Andrea said.

"My grandmother wrote all kinds of children's books. Here's one, and Abby, here's one in Braille."

I read the book quickly and loved it. The stories were so entertaining. She was really a talented writer.

"Here's a picture of my beautiful grandmother," she said and handed the picture to Alison.

"She is simply beautiful," Alison said.

"She has braided hair that she has pinned up on top of her head, a beautiful floppy hat and a really long skirt," Andrea told me.

"Hey Harry, I brought this from the trunk. What is it?" I asked. I handed Harry a small medal.

"Oh, my," Harry said. "This is Melissa's Purple Heart. She was injured in the war when she was pulling soldiers into a tent during combat."

We all oooed and ahhhhed.

"I still don't know why my grandmother stopped writing in her diary," Elizabeth said simply. "She loved to record everything in her life. Well, I guess we'll never know, but she was one great woman and I miss her dearly."

After a really fun afternoon, we thanked Harry and Elizabeth and all gave him big hugs and went home.

"Spies in Disguise"

Later on that afternoon, the gang and I snuck back upstairs to revisit Selma's trunk to see if we could find any more clues that might tell us why she stopped writing. Out-of-the-blue Neils found it.

Before Neils made the "big discovery" we found all kind of cool items from Selma's life.

We put on more clothes, laughed at old hats and shoes. There were also old pictures that were worn from time.

We were having the best time whenever Neils yelled, "I got it."

"You got what?" I asked.

"I knew Selma would not stop writing for no reason. She was a writer and a writer doesn't just abruptly stop writing, so I began looking deeper into the trunk and sure enough I found this."

Neils placed another diary into my hands.

"I looked all through the trunk and didn't find anything," I said.

"There's a secret compartment inside of the trunk. Look here," Neils said.

There it was placed behind the torn cover that held the secret diary and boy did Selma have a secret.

"READ IT NOW," my gang yelled at me.

I grabbed the diary and placed it in my hands, so the mob wouldn't kill me.

Selma began,

"I wonder how long I can keep the secrets for our government without Ben knowing. I am a member of OSS and work behind the scenes for the United States. Since I have traveled to Europe, I was able to go and live with Mare for a year and would decode secrets for our government. I would write what was going on in Braille, so that if I was caught the enemy wouldn't know what I was reading. You see, Braille is different in every language, so I was feeling fairly confident."

Selma continued to explain that once she was captured by the Germans. The soldiers insisted that she decode the Braille secrets to them.

She was able to escape with the help of another American spy. Since Selma was reliable and dependable she was an excellent spy for the United States during the war.

"Selma was a spy!" Alison shouted.

"Yep, and how cool is that!" I screamed. I continued reading.

"Ben is getting suspicious but I keep telling him that Mare is having trouble and I am there to help take care of her.

Ben is such a kind man to understand that I need to help Mare. I cannot jeopardize his or Melissa's life during these war times. Melissa is caring for the soldiers in combat.

I know Ben is lonely, but I will return to him as soon as I can."

"Girls, what are you doing?" Mom asked.

Ooops. We were caught red-handed. Neils was wearing an old flapper dress, Alison had on a really old wedding dress, Andrea and I were wearing pillbox hats and gloves.

"Mom, we found Grandmother Elizabeth's grandmother's trunk."

"Well as long as Mom doesn't mind, then I don't. How did you girls find this room? I didn't know it existed but I kept hearing old jazz music the other day and thought I had lost my mind. Today I heard the laughter and knew I wasn't losing my mind, so I decided to investigate the attic. How neat that there is a secret room. Well, you girls have fun, Chip and I are going shopping."

"Bye Mrs. D," everyone hollered out.

Selma loved working in the secret organization and felt proud to serve her country, but she could never tell anyone.

She told the gang, but we knew how to keep Selma's secret and all of the secrets that were in the attic.

Teenage Wizard

By: Kristie Smith-Armand, M.Ed, TVI

"Magic is believing in yourself.
If you can do that, you can make anything happen"

Joann Wolfgang

"Middle School"

It was the first day of middle school, and I, Abigail Diamond was going to be the coolest, the smartest and the most beautiful girl in the school. I didn't really feel this way about myself but was trying what Oprah calls "self-talk". I walked in the new school, Thomas Jefferson Middle School.

This would be the first time that I would not be in the school where my mom teaches.

At first I felt sad, but then I became glad.

Wow. I get to cut the apron strings and fly, I thought while trying to make myself feel better.

"Abby," Ms. Ashley, my vision teacher yelled. Ms. Ashley.

"I am really glad to see you," I sighed.

"It's nice to be wanted," she laughed.

We walked into my class and Ms. Ashley helped me get situated.

"Hey, Abby, come sit by me," Neils yelled.

I knew that Neils and my buddy Anthony were going to be in my first class with Andrea in my second period, so I was feeling pretty good about middle school already. Anthony, Alexis and I are the only three blind students in our school. Anthony's brother, Aaron, also has a visual impairment. They are all three such cool kids.

"Man, I'm nervous," Neils whispered to me.

"I'm excited," I said proudly.

"You would be Blondie".

Who was talking to me and who was calling me Blondie I wanted to know?

"Excuse me?" Neils and I said in unison.

"Mind your own business, Red," he yelled at Neils.

"What's up with you? Did you forget your medicine this morning?" Neils replied, and then I laughed and laughed hard.

"Hey, Cutie, you don't need that cane, do ya?" quipped the outlaw.

Man, this guy was ruder than Simon Cowell from American Idol.

"Yes, I do," I stammered. "Why do you ask?"

"Oh, I don't know. I just wondered," the bully laughed.

I reached down for my cane, and it was gone.

Ms. Ashley had left the room for a moment but was back by then and heard what was going on.

"Give back her cane, and leave the girls alone," Ms. Ashley yelled.

After a few minutes I heard a whisper in my ear, "You tattle tale." I hated to admit this but I was scared and intimidated by this kid. After class Neils and I started talking.

"Man, Abby. That mean kid's name is Jimmy. He is so rude. My brothers told me to watch out for him. He and his brothers are bad news," Neils continued.

I felt better when I walked into second period right and heard Andrea's sweet voice.

"Abby, I'm coming to sit by you."

I told Andrea all about the mean kid named Jimmy.

I knew he was really bad news and that even the teachers are scared of him.

"I heard that he beat up his bus driver," Andrea said. I felt sick to my stomach when I heard that, so the next two class periods I worried about bumping into the bully.

When it was finally lunchtime, I met up with Ms. Ashley again. She walked me through the line and back to a table with my gang, Madison, Michael, Jessica and the others.

"Middle school is great," I heard Jaxson say.

"Man, we get to eat all kinds of good junk."

Glen the parrot surprisingly agreed, "Yep, yep, yep".

I told Jaxson about Jimmy because, to tell you the truth, I was scared.

"Man, Abby, don't worry about that creep. If he bothers you, I'll clobber his big head with books."

"Yeah," Glenn agreed.

The bell sounded and it was time to go.

I got up from my chair to take my tray by myself because Ms. Ashley had to go to another school.

I thought I was doing pretty well until I stumbled across a massive tennis shoe.

"Watch out, Blonde Girl!" Jimmy screamed at me.

Next thing I knew I fell down hard and could hear Jimmy and his brothers laugh really hard and loud.

As I laid there humiliated and about in tears, Jimmy walked by and "accidentally" dropped his applesauce all over my head.

I cried but was quickly surrounded by my friends and another new boy named Jared.

"Are you okay?" Jared asked me.

"No," I cried.

"Don't worry about anything, Abby. I'll take care of you."

"Thanks Jared. What's your last name?" I asked.

"Jared McCutcheon is my name, and I'm glad to help you out."

"That's more than I can say for Jaxson and Glen. By the way, Neils, where are my Knights -in- Shining Armor?"

"They ran out about the time you had applesauce dripping from your long blond ponytail," Neils stated without missing a beat.

What happened next was simply bizarre my sighted friends told me.

'Ol Mean Jimmy was laughing and pointing at me whenever his mouth became glued shut. He was struggling to open his mouth but couldn't. I then heard a loud splat, and it was Jimmy. Neils told me that he panicked whenever he couldn't speak and began to run when he tripped and slid across the cafeteria and landed in a pile of trash right next to the toothless custodian. I heard someone whisper to me, "I told you I would take care of you."

"Teenage Wizard"

I was stunned, so I just sat there with applesauce dripping across my forehead.

What did Jared mean? He would take care of me? How did he manage to tape the bully's mouth shut?

The next period was fourth. Would this day ever be over?

I heard a sweet sound when I walked into the classroom. It was two of my buddies, Alexis and Alison.

"Abby, oh my gosh. What happened to you?" Alexis asked.

"I was basically tortured and humiliated in the cafeteria," I yelled.

"Abby, you are not the only one," Alexis continued. "Jimmy grabbed my note taker, threw it down, and stomped on my fingers whenever I yelled for help. He's got to be stopped."

Just then I heard the new familiar sound of Jared's voice.

"Abby," he whispered when the kids were taking their seats. "I can cast spells. I use magic to turn wrongs into rights."

"Oh," I stammered and wondered if Jared was completely nuts.

"Don't worry, Abby, I only take care of mean kids. Use your cane as a magic wand after I put a spell on it. You can then take care of yourself whenever I am not around."

"Are you serious?" I asked.

"Yes," was all he said and then took his seat.

"Tiny Bubbles"

After a very restless night of dozing off and one and a night full of nightmares about my old doll Maria that haunted my childhood, I was groggy. I did not want to go to school and felt a very large lump in my throat.

"Abby," my mom screamed, "You need to hurry up before you're late."

Like that would be a disaster- me being late to be tortured and humiliated.

After Ms. Ashley left my first period class, I was using my note taker, printing off my assignments when I heard a voice in my ear.

"Blonde Girl, I ain't done with you, yet."

I froze. I mean I usually have a very smart mouth, but I was scared until I remembered what Jared told me- 'Use your cane as a magic wand'. Why not? What did I have to lose, so I picked my cane up, pointed it in the direction of Jimmy's voice and said quietly, 'Be glued to your seat, Bully'.

When it was time for our class to leave I heard Jimmy scream,

"Help, I'm stuck."

"I would help you, Chump," I said, "but I'm too blonde to do much good. So long lead butt."

The whole class and I laughed and gave each other high-fives.

I bumped into Jared in the cafeteria.

"Hey, Jared. You are too cool. Thanks so much for your help. My cane is teaching the bully a lesson that he will never forget."

"Want to have some more fun with your cane?" he giggled.

"Sure, what is it?" I asked.

"Everyone is drinking something, milk, soda, lemonade, etc. Wave your cane and say the following, "When life gives you lemons make lemonade."

I laughed so hard and did what Jared said. I waved the cane and said the magic phrase.

All of a sudden I heard bubbling all over the cafeteria. Kids began screaming and laughing all at the same time.

"What's happening?" I asked Jared.

"Well, let's just say that there are tiny bubbles all over the cafeteria."

After the bell sounded, Andrea explained everything to me.

"Abby it was so weird. I was just sitting there and talking to Michael when my milk and his lemonade began bubbling all over the place. We then noticed that the whole cafeteria was bubbling. Man, this is such a cool place."

"Math Madness"

I typically do well in school. I mean I use my note taker, printer, laptop, Braille books and my recorder and I'm on my way, until, that is, math time.

I am not what Einstein would call a math wizard. So, there I sat, in math class, on a table with the dumb kids.

Oh, I know Ms. Ashley and my math teacher say it's so "I will understand it better since I can't see", but I don't care how they sugarcoat it, it's still the "Dumb Table".

"Okay, Class," Mrs. Branch began. The problem of the day is. . ."

I already had enough problems dealing with the bully, finding my way around middle school and a multitude of others, so yeah, sure give me another problem.

"Abby, do you have your note taker and Talking Calculator ready," Mrs. Branch asked me.

"Yes, I'm ready." Mrs. Branch continued, "Okay here's the problem."

Then she read the problem really fast and I brailled as fast as my fingers would allow. Shane has 18 blue envelopes. He has 9 fewer yellow envelopes than blue envelopes. He has 5 times as many green envelopes as yellow envelopes. How many envelopes does Shane have? What did I care? I don't even know Shane. I could care less about his envelopes and having fewer and more and blah, blah, blah. Why didn't they ask me about Shane's girlfriend or a bully who is picking on him? Then I might have had an interest.

A new kid named Meredith spouted off the answer. I agreed with Meredith about old stupid Shane's envelopes and shut my note taker.

It was five minutes before math class finally ended. Mrs. Branch was getting ready to give the class an assignment when I had a great idea. Why didn't I use my cane for the good of others? Surely the other kids didn't want homework anymore than I did, so I waved my magic cane and said in a low whisper, "Math homework is a waste of time." It worked.

Mrs. Branch suddenly announced to the class,

"Hmmm. Class, I have suddenly changed my mind. Let's forget homework tonight and for that matter the rest of the week."

Just then Andrea walked over to me and whispered,

"Abby. I saw you wave your cane and mumble something to yourself. Girl, you aren't losing it, are you? Jimmy isn't worth going to the nut house over."

"Oh, Andrea. I'm not as scared of him as I once was. If he gives you any trouble you come and get me, and I'll take care of him for you," I beamed.

"Sure, Abby, I'm still a little worried about you."

The bell rang and math class was finally over.

"Gym Class"

I found out another problem with being in middle school- gym class. When you are in elementary school, you go to class with buddies, to the cafeteria and to gym fully clothed. You play a little, get water, go to the restroom and then go back to your homeroom class- great, huh?

In middle school you get to change your clothes in front of several other girls and change into white shorts, a white t-shirt, socks and shoes, but at least I had Alison in my fourth period.

"Abby," Alison began. "Here's your bag. Hurry we have to change out of our clothes and get into our workout clothes in five minutes."

"Great," I said. "Alison, can anyone see me change?" I asked.

"Only one hundred other girls," she added.

"That's fair," I said. "I have to strip down and pose in front of all of these girls and they are completely safe to change in front of me because I can't see them at all."

"Don't worry, Abby," Alison continued.

"It's not as if anyone is paying any attention to us. Now hurry up, and we will walk out together."

I began changing into my shorts when I heard laughing.

"Nice underwear," laughed a husky voice.

"Are you talking to me?" I asked.

"Yes, I am. I don't know of any other seventh graders wearing Hannah Montana undies," she laughed.

I felt my face turn a scorching red. I wanted this day to be over and be over soon.

"Oh, no, Abby," Alison whispered to me. "Your Hannah Montana undies are showing through your white short," Alison groaned.

"Oh, no," I cried.

We walked out together out of the dressing room and then I heard more laughter.

"Hey, Hannah, the daycare is down the street."

"Are you talking to me?" I asked finally taking up for myself.

"Yes, Hannah," the voice replied.

"Are you making fun of my underwear because you can see it through my shorts?" I asked.

"Yes, Hannah Babytana," the viper whose name was really Molly answered.

"Well, just let me give you a really good laugh," I scoffed, and then even to my surprise, I pulled down my pants and strutted through the gym in my Hannah Montana undies.

Alison and I started laughing.

I heard a loud whistle, and then quickly pulled up my pants.

"You with the cane," the gym teacher barked.

"Come here," she continued.

I grabbed my cane and quietly waved the magic at her while whispering, "Molly caused the trouble, and she should pay."

Much to my surprise and everyone else's, the gym teacher said, "Now, tell me, Abby. Who was making fun of you in the girls' dressing room? It was Molly, correct?" she asked before I even had the chance to snitch on the snob.

"Well, Molly, come here. I just bought a new pair of size 24 gym shorts for anyone bullying other children. Now, go and change into your new shorts and you'll be wearing them for the next week! And here's a belt so that you can really look fashionable," she laughed.

Molly walked by and grunted to me,

"You'll regret this. Watch out for that beautiful blonde ponytail," she growled.

"Oh, I will. Once again, I wish that I could see, so I could see you in your new fashionable shorts. Molly, don't make threats to people who are helpless."

I laughed and couldn't wait to see Jared.

"The End of the Day"

Finally after everything that I had been through all day nothing eventful happened in my last two classes.

I didn't know one soul the rest of the day, but the kids were really nice and helpful. Since the middle school was further away, I would be riding home with Andrea's mother, Mrs. Williams.

"How was middle school?" Mrs. Williams asked sweetly.

I wanted to cry but managed to squeak out, "It was okay." Andrea must have had a better day than I had because she talked nonstop about having several classes with Anthony. I was glad that her day went well because she kept the conversation going, but all I wanted was to go home, get into bed and not come out until I turned eighteen.

Mrs. Williams and Andrea dropped me off and said good-by. Luckily my family was not home yet, so I could gather my thoughts before I allowed myself a good cry in the shower.

After everyone got home we all sat down for dinner. Mom brought in a big box of chicken, potatoes, hot buttered biscuits and banana pudding. So, today could be salvaged, I thought- until they all began chattering about school.

"How was your first day of preschool?" Mom asked Chip.

"It good," Chippy said. "Robby Gween poop in his pants," he innocently said.

I laughed so hard and almost spit out my mashed potatoes.

However, my lighthearted mood did not last.

"Abby, how was your first day of middle school?" my dad asked.

"It didn't go as well as I had hoped," I said, "but I did meet a really cool new kid named Jared," I said.

"Robby Gween poop in his pants," Chippy chirped again.

We started laughing. Gosh, I love that little guy, I thought.

That night I was starting to get nervous again about going back to school. I mean Jimmy and Molly would be there again tomorrow. When I get nervous, I eat, so I went into the pantry and ate four Pop Tarts. Thank goodness, I'm still on the thin side.

"More Bullies"

I wasn't feeling very enthusiastic about going to school the next morning, so I feigned a stomachache.

"Ouch," I cried. "I believe my stomach is upset. I think I need to stay in bed," I determined.

"And how long do you need to stay in bed?" Mom asked in an "I-Don't Believe-You voice".

"Until I'm eighteen," I stated.

"Abby, get up and get going. You cannot run from people or obstacles. You have to find the correct way to stand up to them."

"Can I throw a few punches and plead self-defense?" I asked casually.

Mom began, "Abby, you know what's right in your heart. I don't need to give you the answer to that one."

Darn. I hated when she put the ball back in my court. I was learning to hate the words 'independent' and 'responsibility'. Gross.

I got dressed and waited by the door until I heard Mrs. Williams honk. I walked outside and got into the car for another day of being the victim, but wait, I forgot I had my cane. Thanks to my new friend Jared I would be able to take care of myself.

After Mrs. Williams dropped Andrea and me off, I walked to my locker, used my key and opened it.

Just about that time a voice came up from behind me, "Just because your blind doesn't mean that you have to have a baby lock on your locker?" The bad news was that this voice did not belong to my other two enemies, Jimmy and Molly but to another barbaric boy named Ernesto.

"Excuse me?" I answered with an attitude.

"Don't give me that attitude because I can't see," I snorted.

"Well, I can't see either and I don't have a lock on my locker," Ernesto yelled.

"Wow, what a jerk you are," I answered back.

"Hey, Ernesto," I continued, "If I want a lock on my locker, then I'll put one on. How do you do your locker combination if you can't see?" I asked.

"That would not be any of your business," he croaked.

I was standing there wondering if he was really blind whenever I heard his cane tapping on the floor.

I then heard the worst sound ever and wanted to scream.

"Hey Cutie," the voice said.

Yep, it was none other than my other nemesis, Jimmy.

"Come on Ernesto," Jimmy said, "Let's get away from the tattletale before we start wanting to go to the kindergarten class and sing our ABC's again," he laughed.

I heard both boys' rude laughter.

"Whatever," I scoffed.

Alison then walked up to me.

"Hey, Abby. Did you know that there is another student who can't see on this campus?"

"Yep," I answered in a disgusted voice. "Not only can he not see, he's rude, hateful and runs around with Jimmy. I bet that mean girl, Molly is his girlfriend," I added.

Alison and I walked together because our first period classes were next door to each other.

"Bye, Abby. Have a good day, and try to steer clear of the bullies today," Alison added.

"I'll try," I said, "But my luck hasn't been so great lately."

Before I walked into first period I heard someone scream, "I ain't putting my head in that toilet," and then I heard a flush, screams and mean laughter coming from the boys' restroom. "Hahahahha," echoed some hateful voices.

"What are you looking at?" I heard Jimmy and Ernesto yell towards me.

"I can't see, so I am not looking at you two, and you don't scare me," I yelled back.

Jaxson must have been the bobbing apple in the bathroom because I heard him behind Jimmy,

"You ain't getting away with that, You, You…" I had had enough, so I took out my cane and said some really mean words and 'poof' Jimmy and Ernesto flew back inside the bathroom and I could hear the toilets flushing and them screaming.

"Are you okay, Jaxson?" I asked.

"Yes, Abby. Man I scared the two of them boys, so they must have gone back in that bathroom and dunked their own heads."

"Sure, Jaxson, that's what happened and your welcome."

I walked into my classroom, sat down and placed my head on the hard uncomfortable surface.

"It Isn't All Bad"

Believe it or not, the rest of the day actually got better.

"Hey Abby," I heard a friendly voice call out. It was Jared.

"Hey, Jared," I whispered to him. "You are the nicest new friend that I have met. Thank you so much for the, the," I stammered.

"Your welcome," he whispered sweetly and disappeared around the corner.

At the end of the day, I was at last with my favorite friends, Alison, Andrea, Alexis and Neils.

"Have you met the new kid named Ernesto?" asked Neils.

"He is really cute," Neils gushed.

"Neils, listen to me," I begged. "He's not a nice guy and you need to avoid him," I said firmly.

"Really?" Neils questioned. "Your vision teacher Ms. Ashley and Ernesto were laughing when they were going to work in the Braille room this afternoon. He really seems nice," stubborn Neils continued.

"Mark my word, he's trouble," I said.

Andrea immediately changed the subject.

"Hey guys, there's a school dance next Friday. Are we all in?" she asked.

"Yes," we all said together.

"I am going to buy a new outfit and dance with Ernesto," Neils teased but really meant it.

"Okay, Neils, suit yourself, but don't come crying to me whenever he puts your head in a toilet," I scoffed.

We laughed that uncomfortable laugh, the one when you're trying to stay friendly but are trying to make a point.

Jaxson and Neils walked up with some other great kids, Madison, Melissa, Kelsey, Kandi and Troy.

We were all laughing and talking and planning for a fun night at the dance. I have to admit that for once, since entering the building, I was actually having a good time.

That weekend Nan, Katy, Chip, Brennan and I went shopping. Nan bought me some really cool blue jeans, a sparkled shirt and a great blingy necklace and bracelet.

The night of the dance, Katy fixed my long blonde hair into spiraled curls.

"Be still," Abby she yelled.

"Gosh, that hairspray stinks," I said.

"Just a few more minutes and I will be finished."

"Wow," was all Katy said for a minute.

My mom and dad came into the room after Katy fixed my hair.

"Abby," my mom said. "You are so beautiful."
"Thanks, Mom, I got my looks from my mom," I teased.

My dad drove the gang and me to the dance.

It was in the gym and really loud.

The gym was decorated with all types of colorful balloons and banners. It was the dance before the first football game.

"Abby," Andrea squealed. "I'm so excited.

We are finally growing up."

We were standing around when I heard Neils giggling like a hyena, and then I heard her say the most unbelievable thing ever,

"Sure Ernesto, I would love to dance."

Ernesto? Dance? Oh, no. One of the bullies was entering my social circle.

I was really starting to fret when I heard a voice in my ear,

"Abby, would you like to dance?"

"Who is it?" I asked softly.

"It's me, Michael." My heart stopped a beat.

I had had the biggest crush on Michael for a long time. I was going to be cool and act like a supermodel, but before I knew it, I grabbed Michael's arm and blurted out,"Heck, yes I want to dance." We danced and were having the best time when I bumped into someone behind me.

The voice whispered, "Everyone in your group and our teacher think that I'm a nice guy, so you better get with the program, Girl," the voice said.

Yep, it was Ernesto, so I whispered back,

"Ernesto did you like your swimming lesson the other day and would you like another one?" I asked.

He must not have enjoyed his morning dunk the other day because I didn't hear another word from him the rest of the night.

After the dance we all spent the night with Neils. We talked about all of the kids that were there, ate cheese dip, yum, and wonderful warm chocolate chip cookies.

"Hey Abby, that new kid Jared is really cool but strange," Andrea said.

"I know what you mean, Andrea. He is different for sure, but he's really a fun person to hang with," I said.

"Yeah, and he is kinda cute, too. He has blonde curls and very large brown eyes," Andrea swooned.

Neils's sweet mom laid out blankets, pillows and comforters for us to lie on. We watched movies until really late.

As I was dozing off to sleep I had the sweetest thought of Michael. Growing up had its advantages after all.

"Monday Morning Surprise"

For some reason, I dreaded Sunday nights especially if I was feeling stressed about the next day.

Dad cooked hamburgers on the grill, and I ate two of them. My dad makes the greatest burgers ever.

They have really thick meat and special seasonings that make the burgers delicious!

However, after I eat that much and am dreading the next day, I toss and turn all night.

I have a Talking Watch that speaks its cruel voice to me, "1 am", "2 am" "3 am". When

I woke up the next morning, I felt like I still needed a good five more hours of sleep.

"Abby, hurry up," my mom screamed. "Chippy, stop whining and get dressed," she continued. When Mrs. Williams honked for me, I felt like I had been hit by a Mac truck. Andrea must have felt the same way because whenever I got into the car she grunted a weak, "hi", and I responded with a weak, "hi".

"Wow, you girls still haven't caught up on your sleep from the weekend have you?" We both grunted a no as politely as we could.

I was not ready for the Monday morning surprise that Ms. Ashley had waiting on me when she pulled me out of first period.

"Abby, we are going to share our time with a new student. Ernesto, meet Abby. Abby this is Ernesto," she beamed.

"I have met him," I snorted with disgust.

"Hi Abby, it's nice to meet you," The two-faced bully said.

"Abby, what's wrong with you. Now you behave. You're not the only student who has a visual impairment, so be nice," Ms. Ashley scolded.

"I'm sorry, Ernesto," I grunted. "Nice to meet you," I said. I might as well play along with this creep's game until I can figure out what he has up his sleeve.

"Abby and Ernesto, you two will share our Braille time and Alexis and Anthony will share their Braille time," Ms. Ashley began.

"But, but, I need my own time," I pleaded.

"Abby, that is not going to be possible this year. My caseload is huge. I have twenty-five students, fourteen schools weekly. Now what's up with you today?" she asked.

"I think I'll just keep my mouth shut," said.

"Okay, that's your choice," scoffed Ms. Ashley.

"Now come on you two, and let's get to the Braille room before the end of the period."

We worked on our note takers, printed our work and began reading a hilarious story about a girl who solves mysteries when Ms. Ashley's cell phone rang.

"Ooops, this is the office calling me. I'll be right back."

So, there I was left sitting with someone who might possibly stick my head in the toilet. "

"Abby," Ernesto said quietly.

"Yes," I answered slowly.

"I ain't done with you or your chubby friend, Jaxson yet. I have just begun, so watch out, Chick."

Oh, no he didn't just call me chick. I sat there and waited for my temper to cool when I quietly picked up my cane and whispered,

"Let Ms. Ashley see the real you." Just about that time Ms. Ashley walked into the room.

"Abby, put down your cane, we're not ready to go yet," Ms. Ashley said.

"Yes, put down the cane before I take your cane and throw it up against the wall," Ernesto said in spite of himself.

"Ernesto!" yelled Ms. Ashley. "You apologize now."

"Maybe I will and maybe I won't," he scoffed. "Abby, you wait here. Ernesto and I will be taking a walk to the principal's office."

So off they went down the hallway and into detention land. It was going to be a great day after all or so I thought.

After second period I was digging around in my bag that was inside of my locker whenever someone came up and pushed me aside and slammed my locker shut.

"Here's the little girl who has to cry and tell on everyone," the voice said. It was none other than Jimmy.

"Leave me alone," I cried.

"Weave me awone," he mocked.

Next thing I knew he grabbed my cane from me and threw it to someone who was standing behind him, Ernesto.

"Now, what'cha going to do?" he laughed.

"I think I'll have some fun with you. Hmmmm. Let's see. I know I'll throw down your note taker and then break your printer. That'll teach you to tell on my best friend."

I was getting scared and downright sick at my stomach whenever I heard a pleasant voice behind me, "Abby, are you okay?" It was Jared.

"Listen to this, Abby," Jared whispered. "Girls are made of sugar and spice and everything nice."

The next thing I heard was kids laughing in the hallway, really hard. Neils came up hysterically laughing, "Oh, Abby. That mean kid, Jimmy, is wearing a pink skirt, pink girl cowboy boots, large pink earrings and a sparkled pink top. Man that kid is weird and his buddy, Ernesto is wearing a lady's dress with big blue earrings. Hahaha," Neils laughed.

"I am here for you, Abby," Jared said and continued, "Oh and here is your cane. Hang on to it next time."

The bell rang for my next period class. During my English class the school always does the announcements. Two kids blabbed on and on about due dates for Student Council, etc., so I decided to have a little more fun. I said some magic words for Jimmy and Ernesto. I whispered them quietly and waved my cane. Poof! The two chatterboxes on the announcements began talking about two boys who were parading down the hall in dresses. I could hear loud laughter all over the school. Everyone was going crazy. Neils and I were laughing so hard that my side starting hurting.

After class I was walking down the hall when I felt a foot, and then I tasted the hallway. Yep, it was Jimmy.

"I don't know what you're pulling, Blondie, but enough is enough. How does the hallway taste?" and then the old bully added, "Come on Ernesto, let's go give Jaxson and Glen a "Swirly".

I could hear their loud laughter all the way down the hallway.

"Go, Team, Go"

The rest of the week was not too bad other than the fact that I had to sit in Braille class with Ernesto.

The weird thing was that whenever he was with Ms. Ashley he was a pretty cool kid. It was only when she left the room or if he was with Jimmy that Ernesto made the transformation from good to bad kid.

I had a new Orientation and Mobility specialist who was the coolest person ever. Her name was Ms. Dardis Croom soon to have a new last name after her wedding in July. Mrs. Croom picked me up and took me to find my landmarks around the school.

"Abby, I've been told that you are doing 'weird' things with your cane lately. Is that true?" Ms. Croom questioned.

"Well, um, you see," I started.

"No excuses, Abby," Mrs. Croom said. "The cane is not for play. It's for safety and plus people tell me you are freaking them out mumbling and waving it around. Doing that kind of thing is certainly not age appropriate for a middle school student."

"Yes, I understand," I said and not meaning a word of it.

"Abby, are you going to the pep rally in ten minutes?" Ms. Croom asked me.

"Sure, where is the gym from here?" I asked.

"Well," she said with a smile, "You show me."

So Ms. Croom and I walked to the assembly until I met up with The Four Musketeers.

"Hey Abby, we are over here," yelled Andrea. "I'm coming," I squealed.

This was a really cool thing about middle school.

I loved going to sporting events and hanging out with the kids. I just listened a lot and asked mucho questions.

"Gross," Neils said. "There's that rude girl named Molly. She's cheerleader, beautiful and think she's all that," Neils growled.

"Yea, I mean she bumped into me the other day and told me to get my large behind out of her way," Neils continued.

"I know what you mean," I said. "She laughed at my underwear in gym class just because I was wearing Hannah Montana undies."

"You still wear Hannah undies?" questioned Neils. "Yes, well, I did until I was humiliated," I said.

The cheerleaders came out and did their cheers jumping and shouting and carrying on. What was wrong with me lately? I mean, I did not like Molly, and the more that I thought about what she did to me, the madder I got. I took my cane out and whispered again, and then I heard the whole gym erupt in laughter.

"Tell me," I screamed. "What is happening?" I begged.

"Oh, Abby," Neils laughed. "Molly was being thrown up in the air during the cheer when her skirt fell off, and she was wearing Hannah Montana underwear."

I laughed and laughed, too, but somehow I didn't get a good feeling about what I had done. After all, I was becoming more and more like Jimmy, Ernesto and Molly.

"Braille Time"

One day during my Braille class, Ms. Ashley left the room for a good twenty minutes and left me with Ernesto.

"Why do you pick on me and others?" I asked Ernesto.

"I don't know, Abby. I guess I just want to fit in with someone, and Jimmy lives down the street from me. To tell you the truth that kid is nuts, and I would like new friends."

"Hey, Ernesto, I am having a pool party next weekend. Why don't you come and hang out with us? You are really a cool kid, and I don't like to see you with Jimmy. You are way too much fun to run around with him."

The next week and several weeks after, Ernesto became a part of our gang. Old Jimmy had a hard time with it at first, but he eventually gave up and found another bully to hang out with while at school.

"Jimmy"

The week before our fall break things were hectic due to exams, studying and of course, fun weekend events with my group that was getting bigger every day!

We talked on our cell phones, corresponded on a social network for kids and were having the best time ever- then I got a call.

"Abby, it is a good thing that you can't see what is on my Kidsrock page," Alison told me.

Kidsrock was a social networking service that was online and for kids only.

"What is it?" I asked.

"Well," she stammered, "You, on the floor of the hallway, with your books scattered everywhere. Then there is a remark about blondes not having more fun."

I sat there, without talking, for a long time, and then finally said, "Who did this to me?"

"Molly and Jimmy," was Alison's answer.

I could feel my face growing redder by the minute.

"Yes, they are a couple now," Alison told me. I hung up the phone and was really angry.

Why were these two so out to get me? What had I done to them to make them my enemies?

Even though I knew it was wrong, I was plotting a way on how to get even. Bad Abby, my voice kept telling me, but I chose to ignore it.

"Molly"

The next day at school I was getting ready for gym class.

"I saw your picture on Kidsrock," Molly laughed, "Did you have a nice trip?"

I ignored her for once. I was really trying to be the bigger person.

I heard her squeaky laugh continue and bit my tongue.

"Don't worry about her, Abby," Alison said. "She's got problems."

"Tell me about," I said.

During gym we had to exercise and then jog around the track field. I was jogging when I heard,

"Hey Blondie, I mean Hannah," and then Jimmy's croaky laugh. I lifted my cane and heard Jimmy fall on the rough turf.

It's the kind of black tar that you can smell miles away on a hot blistering day.

"You did this to me," he screamed.

"Man, leave the girl with the beautiful blonde hair alone," said a kid.

"She can cast spells," he squeaked sounding more and more like the moron that he was.

I could hear a group gather around Jimmy, and they began to tease him. I was not feeling good about any of this and felt partially to blame.

"Come on, guys. Leave him alone," I begged.

"The girl's coming to your rescue," laughed some deep voices that I did not recognize. I heard some pushing, yelling, and then a whistle blew. Thank goodness, Coach Burke was coming to the bully's rescue.

"Let's break this up," he hollered.

"Everyone to the showers, and I'll talk to all of you guys once we are inside the gym."

When the day was finally over, I went straight home and collapsed in bed. There were parts of middle school that I loved and parts that were simply exhausting.

"Life is But a Dream"

The following day was hump day, the middle of the week. Middle school was turning out to be one good and bad experience.

I was walking down the hall going to my second period class when a hand grabbed my mouth. It was Jimmy.

"You won't get away with humiliating me," he screamed in my ear.

He then took my ponytail and tied it through the hole in a locker combination.

"Don't worry about class," he laughed. "I'll tell the teacher that you are all 'tied up'."

I then heard his loud evil laugh.

I was trying desperately to get my hair untangled when I felt a hand gently reach up to help me.

"Thank you so much," I said. "Some bully tied me up here."

"No problem," the small voice said.

"I want to untie you. Here let me help you."

I reached down to feel of the hand and screamed. It was a cloth hand and a cold ceramic face. My doll Maria had returned. I screamed and screamed loudly. Next thing I knew my mom was shaking me and waking me up.

"Abby, you had onions again, didn't you? Now go back to sleep because tomorrow is your first day of middle school."

Abby Diamond's

"Ghost Tales from Savannah"

"The First Day of School"

It was the first day of a brand new school year.

All of my buddies and I were standing by the tree.

I was still a little groggy because I'm always too excited or scared to sleep the night before school starts.

I am always worrying about who my teacher will be. This year, Mom told me that I was getting a brand new teacher named Mr. Cummings. Mr. Bryce Cummings, to be exact, was none other than the son of Mrs. Cummings our great principal from elementary school. Mr. Cummings must have gotten out of his car when Neils, Alison and all of the sighted girls began screaming.

"What's wrong?" I asked. "Nothing," Andrea said.

"Absolutely nothing. Mr. Cummings is great to look at Abby. I really wish you could see him. He has dark hair and big blue eyes. WOW!!!" oozed Neils who normally never says anything about boys.

The bell rang, and it was time for us to go inside.

I was worried because, good-looking or not, Mr. Cummings would probably not be ready for a blind student.

Even my favorite teachers from the past have always freaked out whenever they hear that I'm coming into their classrooms. Oh, I know that it's nothing personal but geez.

"Everyone, sit down, please," Mr. Cummings said firmly, but nicely. "Abby, I have your work brailled for the week. I've been in contact the past week with your Braille teacher, Ms. Ashley. So, here's your work for today."

"Thanks, Mr. Cummings," I said politely.

I think at that moment I was falling in love, too, just like the other girls.

Mr. Cummings told us to open our journals and write anything that we wanted to write. Neils giggled and read to me her journal after fifteen minutes of writing.

"Abby, my journal says, 'I love Mr. Cummings. Mr. Cummings plus Neils. Hahahha. I'm hilarious."

"Yes, you are Neils. But we are in middle school, so we need to grow up."

I was really glad that I had a note taker that brailles at this very moment. I quickly shut my note taker because, written in Braille, I also wrote that I loved Mr. Cummings.

"Kaitlyn's Surprise"

We were all really enjoying our new teacher, Mr. Cummings and our class. You know how some years everything just seems to fall in place? You have all of your friends in your class and a cool teacher and get to go to PE at the end of the day.

This was going to be my year. But as usual, I was not going to escape another exciting mystery.

It was Friday at the end of the school day, when the bell rang. I packed up my note taker, my tape player and all of my big bulky Braille books.

"Hey Abby," Alison called. "What are you doing over the fall break next weekend?"

"Well, the only thing that I've heard my parents talk about is me raking leaves. What are you going to do?" I asked.

"I wanted to ask you and the gang something together, so wait right here," she said with a smile in her voice.

The gang came over and Alison began, "Okay, you guys know that my mom is constantly feeling guilty for leaving me with Audie."

We shook our head in agreement and grunted.

"Well, this time it will be to all of our advantage if y'all can come with me to Charleston, South Carolina."

"Where is that?" Neils asked.

"It's a really cool place," Andrea added. "I went three years ago, and it has cool beaches, a market place, horse and buggy rides and all kinds of fun stuff to do."

"Yea," Alison agreed. "My mom is filming another movie there and has asked Audie, me and all of you to come along for the long weekend. She is, of course, going to pay for everything."

We were so excited and began 'high-fiving' each other.

"Go home and ask before you get too excited," Andrea beamed.

"What's going on?" asked our new friend, Alexis Cooks.

Alexis was a lot like me. She is smart, funny, intelligent, and modest, and she also had a visual impairment.

We really bonded when we both went to the Texas School for the Blind on the bus. Up until Alexis came to our school, I was the only student who had a visual impairment.

"We're going to Charleston with Alison if our parents agree," I said.

"Hey Alexis, want to come along?" Alison asked. "HECK, YES!" Alexis yelled.

We all cracked up laughing because she said it in such a loud voice. Alexis was so much fun to be around and so nice to everyone that she was quickly turning into the fifth musketeer. That night we were all on the phone back and forth with each other.

All five of our parents agreed because Alison later told us that Audie would go along with us.

"We are getting our own room, just like we had in Galveston with Nan and Pop," Andrea squealed.

"I can't wait to go," I said.

My little brother Chip, that I adore, was somewhat getting on my nerves lately. He was getting into the 'terrible twos' and believe me, it was not much fun to be around the little guy for long. He screams, "Mine", all of the time. He tortures our poor little dog by picking her up, grabbing her ears and pretending to eat her dog food. So, as I said, I'm due for a fun vacation with my best friends.

"The Plane Ride"

The next morning Audie drove himself and the five of us to what would be yet another frightening adventure.

We parked and then carried our luggage to the curb where the bell hop checked us in.

"Are the two of them blind?" Goofy (my nickname for him) the bell hop asked.

"No, why do you ask," Alexis answered.

"Well, you have canes," he blubbered.

"We carry canes so that we can fight the boys off of us you dweeb," Alexis scoffed.

We laughed so hard and began hooting and hollering so loud that Audie told us to simmer down.

As I walking through the tunnel to get on the airplane, a little girl who sounded really small sweetly asked why my eyes couldn't see.

"Well," I started, "God makes us all special but he made Alexis and me extra special."

"That's cool," said the little girl.

My answer must have satisfied her because she didn't say anything else until we were getting on the plane when she said, "Bye-bye, Special Girls" to Alexis me. We boarded the plane and got ready for Charleston. But was it ready for us?

"Charleston, South Carolina"

When the plane landed, Kaitlyn was there to pick us up, and boy was there a commotion. Remember she's a big wig movie star and everybody knows her.

Alison told Alexis and me that Kaitlyn was trying to hide from the cameras, but they found her in spite of her dark sunglasses and baseball hat where her hair was tucked neatly inside.

"Girls, I'm so glad that you could make it. Hi Alexis. I'm Alison's mother, Kaitlyn Somers."

"I've heard of you," Alexis said. "You are rich and famous. I have also heard how beautiful you are." "Why thank you, Alexis. And by the way, you're beautiful yourself."

We got into Kaitlyn's limousine with her fancy driver and drove through the crowd of people screaming out her name. I could hear the shouts of people and the clicking of the camera.

"What's it like to have people love you and want to be like you all of the time," asked Neils.

"Oh, Neils. It's not as much fun as you would think. I can't go anywhere without people taking my picture. The next day I will sometimes read hateful things about me. It's really hard to put up with some days."

Just about then, we pulled up to our hotel.

We were staying right beside the market place in Charleston. The hotel was really big from the sounds that I was hearing.

When the hotel manager saw Kaitlyn he rushed over and introduced himself to her.

"Hello," he stammered.

Since I couldn't see him and could only hear him, I pictured a dork wearing out of style clothes with a bad complexion. He was chattering and making a total fool of himself.

"Would you mind taking our suitcases up to the suites," Kaitlyn asked politely.

"Yes, Ms. Somers," Sponge Bob squeaked.

Finally, we were up in our rooms. I mean our very, very large rooms. The beds were so soft, and the bathtub and room were huge.

Neils, Alison, Alexis, Andrea and I had one very enormous room all to ourselves while Audie had one enormous room to himself.

"I'm not going to complain about this," I heard him chuckle.

"Girls, before I leave, I'm giving each of you a credit card with a thousand dollar limit. Since I've already paid for the room this is your own money for food, fun and souvenirs."

"WOW!" we thanked Kaitlyn and gave her a big hug.

"Alison, I've got to get to the movie set, but Audie said that you will be going to dinner and then on a ghost tour tonight.

Tomorrow, you will come to the movie set, go shopping at the market place and then tour some really cool Civil War homes in the area. Okay. Gotta go. Love you."

I heard her blow a kiss and shut the door behind her.

"Gosh, I love that woman," Neils said.

"Now what's this about a ghost tour?" Alexis wanted to know.

"It will be fun, Alexis. The tours in Charleston are really cool."

"Okay," agreed Alexis reluctantly, "but only because I'm on vacation."

"Now, let's go and see what kind of mystery we can solve while we are here and remember- "What happens in Charleston, stays in Charleston," I laughed and everyone agreed.

That night everyone got ready for a night out in Charleston.

It was warm there just like it is in Texas around this time of year, so I put on a new baby blue sundress with flip-flop sandals and took my small purse that goes across one side of my body to the other side.

"Wow, Abby," Alison said. "You look so pretty tonight."

"Thanks, Alison, I'm sure you do, too, but since I can't see, I'm only speculating."

"Abby, you are so funny," laughed Alexis.

We ate at really cool seafood place near the water by Foley Beach. Audie said that we could go swimming on the beach this week, too.

I ordered my favorite, fried shrimp, french-fries, hot buttery hushpuppies with a glass of sweet tea. After all, I am a true southern girl. Alexis and Neils both ordered hot steaming catfish with fries, hushpuppies and cole slaw while Alison and Andrea got exactly what I ordered. Audie must have loved his "gross-out" oysters, but I refused to even taste one.

"Oh, come on, Abby. It just slips right down your throat," Audie laughed.

"Gross," I laughed.

Alexis was the brave one though. She tasted one oyster and spit it out.

We laughed so loud that Audie said people standing around us began laughing, too.

We walked outside and I could smell the fresh salty smell of the ocean and could feel the hot sun on my back. I didn't want anyone to know, but I was really getting freaked out by the ghost tour.

"I am so excited about the ghost," Neils squealed.

"Me, too," I said and not convincingly even to my own ears.

"Abby, it'll be fun," Neils added. "There's no such thing as a ghost."

Just about that time a woman walked up and introduced herself to the five of us outside the restaurant.

"Hi, Girls," she said. "Are you all tourists?"

"Yes," I said. "We are here visiting friends."

"Well, you will love Charleston. There is so much history from the Civil War as well as the American Revolutionary War. Let me introduce myself. My name is Zoe."

"Hi Zoe," we all answered.

"Are you from around here," asked Audie.

"Oh, yes. I've been here for many many years. I love when tourists come to our town. You will have to try the market place, go on some fun ghost tours and please go and take tours of the old homes. There's so much history in the homes of the original Charlestonians. You mustn't forget to eat at Poogan's Restaurant. The food is delicious and the company is even better."

Zoe then let out a loud contagious laugh. We laughed, too, even though we didn't know what we were laughing at.

We stood around and talked to Zoe for a long time. She was such a nice lady, but when she walked away from us Alison said to Alexis and me, "She looks weird to me."

"Why do you say that?" asked Alexis.

"Well, she has really white skin and bright red lips. You think living near the beach she would have some color."

"Maybe," Andrea continued, "she has such light skin because skin cancer is on the rise, so if you live near the beach you really have to wear your sunscreen."

We agreed, and then Audie yelled for us to board the car and get ready for our first ghost tour. My hands began to shake.

"Lacy and Laura"

We signed up for the first ghost tour at our hotel. I say first because we ended up trying to solve another mystery by listening to the voices of ghost, throughout the streets of Charleston. We lined up against the black wrought iron fence that faced a beautiful church and a cemetery. I got the creeps just knowing what was behind me.

"I don't know if I want to do this," Alexis said in a low whisper.

"Me, either," I replied. "Let's stick together."

Our tour guides were two women who were best friends and did the tours for fun and extra money.

"Just call me Lacy and me Laura," the two said. According to Neils, Lacy was a blonde haired beauty with large green eyes. She told Neils that she also sang country music. Laura was a dark haired stunner with dark brown eyes who was studying to be an actress.

Both girls had the best laughs ever. Every time we heard them laugh we would naturally join in with them.

The girls told us that they loved doing the tours when they were home in Charleston for the holidays.

We walked next to the fence pretending to see or hear things that we really didn't.

We learned about a famous ghost mother whose child died at birth. The two future stars told us that if we listened or looked really hard we could see her by the tombstone.

"I don't care how hard I look, I ain't seeing nothing," I said. Alexis and I both laughed hard at my joke. I could hear other people in the group snickering, too. It seemed that this tour was so boring that I would have to be the entertainment. That soon changed.

We walked through the streets of Charleston and to a placed called Poogan's Porch Restaurant.

"Hey, that's the place that the nice lady told us about," Audie said.

What the girls told us next made all five of us gasp.

"Zoe"

The two girls began speaking of a ghost that frequently haunts the restaurant.

"The ghost that lives here lived with her sister until she died in the 50's," Laura said.

"If we summon her, maybe she'll appear."

What Laura said next scared the life out of me.

"Zoe, Zoe, appear!"

I heard Alexis scream.

"What is it?" asked Alison.

"Alexis are you okay?"

"I felt something move next to my arm when she said the word Zoe. It was a warm feeling."

When I heard Alexis say that, I panicked and screamed.

I dropped my cane and began running.

Now as you know, I am blind and cannot see anything, so the only thing that stopped me from running out in front of a car was a friendly little tree branch. Whack! I ran into the tree so hard that I fell backward and fell hard.

"Abby," everyone screamed. "Are you alright?"

"Here, Abby. Let me have a look at you," Audie said.

"I am okay, I think," I lied.

I was still scared that Zoe was probably standing next to me just waiting to take a bite out of me or something. The whole tour stopped and Laura and Lacy came over to me.

"Are you okay? We didn't mean to frighten you. You see, Zoe is really a very friendly ghost. She won't hurt you."

"Well, thank you, girls, but I think we'll be heading back to the hotel," Audie told them.

On the way back to the hotel, Audie wanted to know why we screamed when we heard the name Zoe.

"Don't you remember, Dad," Alison said.

"That's the lady that we met at dinner. She told us to go to this restaurant."

"Oh, come on, Alison. Y'all don't really believe that that's the same Zoe, do you? Girls, there's no such thing as a ghost and there's a logical explanation for this. I am sure of it."

"Okay, Audie," I said, "If you think everything's okay then I believe you."

To calm us down, we went to the really cool market place and all bought purses.

"What color is this?" asked Alexis.

"Yours is a beautiful turquoise, and Abby's purse is a gorgeous dark purple," answered Andrea.

"Great. What else can we buy?" If you remember from my past experiences that my nana is a shop 'til you drop kind of lady, and I have inherited that gene from her."

The next really cool place that we went was a dress place made especially for Charleston. We had so much fun in this shop.

Alison told me that she bought a beautiful baby blue dress with sparkles, matching blue earrings and another purse. Andrea bought a really short cute black and red dress with black sparkled shoes and funny Neils bought a really cool green army-colored combat type shirt with a matching skirt. Audie said that she really fit the scene in Charleston.

That night we were exhausted. The five of us put on our pajamas, went to bed and giggled until we feel asleep but not for long.

"The Middle of the Night"

I was enjoying a really cool dream about getting married. I was marrying my dream guy, Brock that I see yearly at Texas School for the Blind. Brock and I were just about to tie the knot when I heard a whisper in my ear, "You're too young to marry."

"Whhat?" I stammered. "Who is there?"

"It's me, Zoe. Next time you'll miss the tree branch and end up in front of that car." She began laughing a really loud, scary laugh.

I jumped up and tried to run but my legs were too heavy. I felt a hand grab me and pull me from the floor, and then I screamed.

"More Ghost Tours"

"Abby, what's going on?" screamed the other four girls.

"Are you okay?", "Did you eat onions tonight? They always give you nightmares."

"I am okay, gang. I was having a really good dream when Zoe whispered in my ear. I know it was her. I could feel her breath in my ear," I said.

"I know what you mean," said Alexis. "That happened to me last night."

"There's only one way to solve this," said Andrea. "

"Neils, call the front desk and ask about more ghost tours."

"More ghost tours?" Alexis and I screamed.

"Are you crazy?" I asked.

"No, just being practical," said Andrea. "I'm with Audie and I still do not believe that the Zoe we met and the Zoe from the ghost tour are one in the same. Besides I won't believe in ghosts until something or someone proves otherwise." There's Andrea, always the practical one and then there's me- the paranoid one.

"Okay," I stiffened. "I want to go on another tour that will talk about Zoe. I want to find out all I can about her."

Neils called the front desk, and we heard about another cool walking ghost tour. Some lady named Trisha was going to lead us, but in the meantime we were going on some normal Civil War home tours.

"Charleston's Beauty"

The next morning after an obvious restless night, Audie took us to a wonderful brunch served at our hotel. I ate hot scrambled eggs with buttered toast and a big gooey cinnamon roll. After we ate, Audie took us on a wonderful carriage ride through the streets of Charleston.

We filled the carriage, so we got the carriage to ourselves. Kaitlyn surprised us that morning and went along with us. She also invited us to her movie set the next day.

"Wow, Mom. People are really staring again," Alison worried.

"It's okay, Allie. Let them stare. I'll be more worried when they don't stare because then I probably won't be able to treat my daughter and her buddies on fun trips like this one." She hugged Alison and me.

"Then, let them stare," I said.

Our driver, Steve was really cool.

He told us that he had a master's degree and worked at the college. He drove the carriage for fun and extra money. Steve took us down Battery Street where Neils and Andrea described all the neat homes to Alexis and me.

"There's a pink house, Abby," Neils laughed.

"It's really pretty and looks like you lick off the icing."

"You crack me up," I told Neils.

Steve told us when the Civil War began the homes in Charleston became occupied by the southern soldiers because the bombs were too far off to completely destroy some of the beautiful mansions.

"What was the Civil War about?" asked Neils. "

"Neils, Girl, don't you ever listen in class?" Andrea laughed. "You have got to get away from Jaxson during history. You, see the southern people had slaves brought over from Africa to clean for them and do major work with no pay or benefits. I know a lot about this because I am an African American," Andrea boasted. "Anyway, the northern people thought that slavery was inhumane and cruel, which it was. This all happened when President Abraham Lincoln was in office. Remember he did the famous speech called the Gettysburg Address?"

"Sure," was all Neils could say.

"Let me go on," Andrea stated. "The north fought the south, and our country completely split apart. That's why that war was called a civil war because we were fighting each other. The north, of course, won and slavery was over, but we African Americans have always had to fight for our rights."

"Wow," I said. "Andrea you need to be a teacher. I've learned more from you and Steve than I have all of these years in school," I said.

After the exhilarating carriage ride through Charleston, we went on walking tours of the Civil War homes. Even though my feet and my cane's feet hurt, it was so much fun to go where actual slave quarters were and see, or in mine and Alexis's case, feel old equipment and even an old carriage from 1861.

"Audie, can we go on another ghost tour?" I asked after the home tours.

"Why, yes, Abby, but I am afraid that it'll scare you too bad. I don't want you having nightmares every night while you're here."

"Oh, don't worry, Dad," Alison added. "Abby likes hearing about Zoe."

"Abby, as long as you know that the ghosts really don't exist. Remember this is all in fun," Audie said.

"Sure, Audie. Can we go?" I asked again.

"Yes. I'll see what I can find out."

"I already found a cool one," added Neils.

"Sounds good to me," Audie said. "Enough talk about our invisible friends. I'm starved, so let's go eat." I agreed as my stomach growled making everyone laugh.

After we ate at a great sandwich shop where I had the most incredible chicken salad sandwich ever, we went back to the market place much to Audie's chagrin.

"Hey Guys," I said. "My feet hurt, so I am going to sit on this bench."

"Abby, I'll join you. My feet are hurting, too," said Alexis.

Alexis and I sat down on the bench while properly placing our canes under the bench when we heard a slightly familiar voice.

"Hello, girls. It's me, Zoe. Are you enjoying your time in Charleston?"

I wanted to scream but didn't because, after all, there were thousands of people around us. I wondered if they could see Zoe.

"Are you a ghost?" Alexis blurted out. No answer. "I said, are you a ghost?" Alexis said even louder. "Abby, where did she go?"

"I don't know," I answered.

"I think that the ghost is trying to frighten us but whoever or whatever she is, we're going to get behind this and soon."

Just about that time Andrea ran up to us.

"Abby, Alexis and I just saw Zoe. She asked me how I liked Charleston. I got so scared that I ran off," Andrea panted.

"I know," I said. "Alexis and I saw her, too. We are not giving in to this ghostly creature," I said more boldly than I had felt. That night I changed into my blue jeans, sandals and Hannah Montanna t-shirt that I loved that had bling all over it. I pulled my long blonde hair up into a pony tail. Alexis told me that she was wearing her jeans, too with a beautiful sparkled pink top that she bought at the market.

Neils bought another combat army shirt while Alison and Andrea wore their new skirts with t-shirts.

We met again at the cemetery and met our unique tour guide, Trisha.

Trisha was wearing a pirate's uniform. Trisha told us that pirates were a problem years and years ago and that the most notorious one was a pirate named Blackbeard who lived back in the early 1700's. Blackbeard was very tall and wore a beard that covered his face. He carried guns and swords while robbing small merchant ships, and he braided his beard and tied black ribbons on the end. Blackbeard's ghost, luckily, she said, is in North Caroline looking for his head.

"Oh, my gosh!" Alison said and sounded like she might faint.

Finally, the rest of the tour group was ready.

Trisha was a great tour guide. She began teaching us all about the dead in the cemetery and what their fate was. During the tour Trisha began speaking in a Jamaican accent,

"Did y'all ever hear of the saying, 'Saved by the Bell'? She whined and continued, "The bell was put in the coffin years ago just in case the person was not really dead. They would ring the bell if they were still alive so that people could here them as they walked by."

"Oh, my gosh," Alison moaned again.

Poor Alison. She was the one struggling tonight, but I wasn't struggling. I was mad at the old ghost. I wanted to find out all that I could about this pest.

We finally approached Poogan's Porch. "So this is where the old spinster Zoe," I thought.

"Well, come on, Sister. I'll take you on."

I hoped that Zoe couldn't read my thoughts.

Trisha began again, "Poogan's Porch is the best and oldest restaurant that you can visit in Charleston," she said.

"Zoe St. Amand lived her with her sister until her death in 1954. Since that time Zoe has thrown pots and pans and chairs. People have spotted her wearing her long black dress from across the street. Poogan was a little scruffy dog that lived in the neighborhood. He used to run around the neighborhood and beg for scraps. When the restaurant opened, he was the first one to greet the customers. Since his death in the 70's, some people say that they have seen his ghost, too."

"Oh, my gosh," Alison shrieked. "A ghost dog? I have heard it all now."

I kept quiet because I didn't want to feel or hear Zoe. Trisha began again, "Zoe, Zoe, come out so the folks can see you."

"What's happening?" I whispered to Neils.

"Not a dang thing," she whispered back. Just then everyone screamed.

"What's going on?" Alexis screamed.

"The curtains inside the restaurant began moving like crazy," Andrea screamed.

"Help us, Audie," I yelled.

"Now, Girls. The air probably just turned on in the restaurant. You don't really believe this stuff, do you?" We stood their speechless.

"Okay. We've had a great time, but there will be no more ghost tours on this trip. Let's go buy some beach clothes and hit the beach tomorrow."

We all agreed and went back to the hotel.

"Foley Beach"

We packed the sunscreen, towels and ice chest and headed to Foley Beach. It was wonderful and so relaxing after Trisha's tour.

I lay in the sun with Alexis and Alison while Neils and Andrea rode the waves on a boogie board.

Audie sat under the umbrella and read a really cool book about a blind girl that solves mysteries.

After we relaxed and ate, we went souvenir shopping at all of the cool beach stores.

"Hey, I'm almost out of money," Neils said.

"Neils what have you bought besides combat clothes?" I asked.

"Well, I also bought some great pirate stuff."

"Oh, yes, I remember when we were in Galveston, Texas how much you liked the pirate clothes. You are hilarious," I laughed.

Later that night, Kaitlyn met us and took us around the movie set in Charleston.

"What's the movie about?" asked Alison.

"Well, it's a Civil War movie. It's really cool. I get to wear all of the old dresses, hats and shoes. I love acting and being someone else besides myself," Kaitlyn said. "I would love to be you," said Neils. "I mean you are a big time movie star and rich."

"Oh, Neils, trust me, there's much more to life than money and fame. One day you'll understand."

Out of the blue Neils blurted out, "Do you believe in ghosts?"

"What?" Kaitlyn questioned. "Neils, why would you ask such a thing?"

I jumped in and told Kaitlyn the whole story.

Audie had gone back to the hotel room, so I explained what he thought.

Kaitlyn answered, "Hmmm. Girls wait here. I want you to meet someone."

We waited and then Kaitlyn introduced us to a ghost.

"Meet Zoe"

I heard Alison freak out.

"Mother! What are you doing with this ghost?" Alison shrieked.

"Alison, girls I want you to meet Zoe, also known as Karis."

"What are you talking about?" we all asked in unison.

"Karis is an actress. Have you met her?"

"Yes," Karis the friendly ghost replied. "Kaitlyn, I didn't know these girls knew you?"

Kaitlyn continued, "Girls, Karis is an actress. She is paid to act the role of Zoe. She wears the long black dress and walks the streets to drum up business for the restaurant," Kaitlyn said.

"Wow, what a great job," I said.

"I want to be Blackbeard and scare the fire out of people," joked Neils.

This is the day that Neils got her new nickname, Blackbeard.

"Home Again, Home Again, Jiggety Jig"

After our fun trip to Charleston it was time to go to back to school. The fall break was over, but our memories of Zoe and Charleston would last forever.

The next day at school we were all telling Jaxson and his buddy, Glen about our trip and all of the ghost stories.

"Man, I ain't scared of no ghosts," said Jaxson the English major.

"Whatever," I scoffed.

The bell rang and we went into the classroom.

"Blackbeard"

I was sitting in class trying to keep up with Mr. Cummings on my note taker and trying not to think about how much I loved him whenever I heard Jaxson screaming. My heart jumped out of my chest.

"Jaxson!" I screamed. "Are you okay?"

"Help me, help me," he cried.

I then heard a loud thump and what sounded like a baby crying.

"What is going on?" Neils was laughing so hard that she could barely speak.

"Wake up, Jaxson," Neils laughed.

This time it was Jaxson having the nightmare instead of me. I joined the rest of the class laughing and relieved that he was okay.

The next day when I went to class I was unloading my Braille folders when I felt someone's hot breath on me.

"Abby, it's me Zoe."

"What? You're an actress and not real. I'm not scared of you and you're like Blackbeard. You are a dream. Where's my old haunted doll, Maria? Is she about to jump out at me and yell, 'boo'?" I went on.

"No Abby. You are not dreaming. I will see you soon."

Just then.... Mr. Cummings told me to hand in my homework. Mr. Cummings looked over my writing assignment and commented, "Abby, you sure have a great imagination. I must go to Charleston, take a ghost tour and meet Zoe. Looks like you have another "A"."

Aloha

"Trouble In Paradise"

"Project Sea Life"

After the trip to Charleston I did not think that I would ever have another trip that was as much fun or mysterious as that one. After all, when would I ever get to travel again with my best friends and a brand new musketeer, Alexis?

Well, once again I was wrong. I was not prepared for what was about to happen to my friends and me. The next trip, mystery and adventure that we were about to embark on would be one that we would remember forever.

It all began when Neils, Andrea, Alexis, Alison and I joined a new club that was held after school called Project Sea Life. Project

Sea Life was a really cool club for kids to help preserve the oceans and its inhabitants such as the sea turtle, certain types of fish and corals and many other living things.

Project Sea Life was started by a fun kid in our class named Anthony who, like Alexis and me is totally blind and lead by our fun reading teacher Mrs. Bossart.

I had known Anthony for years because we had been in the same class every year in a row and also attended Texas School for the Blind. He was funny, very cute and smart.

Anthony, Alexis and I began working on our note takers together with a really cool technology teacher named Mr. C. Mr. C is surprisingly strong.

He took the bulky brailler and broke it into. I mean just like that. Anthony, Alexis and I were shocked.

"Wow," Anthony said, "Mr. C. did you really break the brailler with your own hands?"

"Now would I lie to you, Guys," asked Mr. C.

"No," I said, "But you can sure tease us like there's no tomorrow." Mr. C laughed and then got really serious like he always does when we start to work with our note takers.

Anthony got Alison really interested in preserving sea life. Alison was from California and lived right near a beautiful blue beach with thick white sand, so she already had a strong interest. Alexis and I wanted to hang out with the gang and Andrea and Neils may have had a slight crush on Anthony. Whatever the reason that we all joined the club, we meet every Wednesday afternoon, and we became very interested in saving sea life.

In Texas the nearest coastline is the Gulf of Mexico. Even though the water is not blue according to the sighted there was still an interest in keeping the coastlines clean and preserving sea life in Texas.

We were, however, not the only kids in this particular club. There were kids from all over the world that were involved in Project Sea Life.

"The Sea Turtle is an animal that has been endangered because of man, pollution and many other factors," Anthony began. "I've made Sea Turtle buttons for everyone to wear," he said.

Andrea helped Anthony pass out the buttons.

I had never seen her so interested in helping a boy before but whatever.

Week after week we were all researching endangered sea animals, writing to our government officials about what could be done and like I said earlier really getting into Project Sea Life.

"Waikiki... WOW!"

My mother and dad were really impressed that our group was so into this project.

"Abby, I am so glad to see you interested in helping the environment and thinking about others like you do. I can tell that you and your friends are growing up. I talked to Alison's mother the other day on the phone about Project Sea Life. We want to do something special for the group because of all of the good that the group is doing," my mom stated.

"Mom, we enjoy the group so much. It makes us feel better to do something good for the environment. After all, how many days can we really shop 'til we drop"? I laughed.

"Abby, promise me you won't tell a soul what I am about to tell you, promise?"

"What, Mom?" I screamed.

I could tell by her voice that this was going to be something great.

"Abby," my mom began, "Kaitlyn has been so thrilled about you and the other children for being involved with Project Sea Life that she is paying for the whole group to go on a six day field trip to Honolulu, Hawaii."

I screamed and then I hugged my mom tightly.

"Wait until after six o'clock tonight," Mom sang. "After six o'clock Kaitlyn will have called all of the other parents, so everyone will know by then."

I was so excited that I could have exploded, but instead I went outside and turned cartwheels.

After dinner, my cell phone began ringing. It was first Neils.

"Abby, oh my gosh!" she screamed loudly in my ear. "I am so excited!"

"Really," I said sarcastically, "I couldn't tell."

I laughed out loud. We began singing hooting and hollering when there was a knock on the door. "Knock, knock, knock".

The knocking was loud and then I heard Mom open the door and in came Anthony and Andrea clapping and hugging me.

"I can't believe we are going to Hawaii," Anthony beamed.

"Me either," I said.

"Man, Kaitlyn's mom is so cool," Anthony continued. "I know," Andrea said and continued,

"She is this really cool movie star with lots of money, but she takes out the time and money to make sure Alison and her friends get to go on the coolest field trip ever," Andrea beamed.

We quickly got on the web and began searching Honolulu, Hawaii. We were told that we were going to stay at the Hyatt Regency right in front of Waikiki Beach. From the oooo's and ahhhhh's that I kept hearing from Andrea as she looked at pictures on the website, I figured this was going to be one special trip that we would never forget.

"Hello Oahu"

The day before we left for the trip, Mom, my little brother, Chip, Nan and I went shopping.

I was so excited that I was getting on everybody's nerves. Even little Chip who adored me stuck his tongue out at me.

"Where can I buy a hula skirt and a coconut bra?" I laughed. I giggled, talked and acted silly all day until Nan asked Mom to take her home, so that she could rest.

"I can't help it," I squealed. "This is my dream vacation. I'm excited and a little nervous. After all," I blabbed, "It is an eight and a half hour flight from here."

"Abby, you'll be fine," Nan reassured me. "Just put on your headphones like you always do anyway and tune everything else out."

"Great idea, Nan," I said.

The rest of the day I tried to control my behavior but it wasn't easy. I did get the coolest clothes ever.

We bumped into Anthony at one of the hottest stores around and he was buying a Hawaiian shirt that was black and white with flowers all over it.

"Aloha," Anthony laughed when he saw me.

"Aloha," I laughed back.

I also bought new jeans, capris, three nice dresses for Texas summer and many t-shirts. Since I already had three bathing suits and a cover up, I was able to buy more clothes for my trip. When we were shopping I talked to Neils, Alison, Alexis, Andrea and Neils four more times.

"Abby, I am so excited that my stomach hurts," Neils joked.

"Me, too. I can't wait to get there. I just wish that we didn't have to take that long airplane ride."

"Kinsy"

After a restless night because of my excitement, I woke up, grabbed my suitcase and small carry-on and waited on Mr. Williams, Andrea's dad to take us to the airport. "Honk, honk", went his Mercedes.

"Bye Chip, bye Mom, bye Dad," I squealed and tried to run out the door.

"Wait a minute," my dad laughed. "You can't leave your old man without hugging him first."

"Yes, and your old woman," my mom joked.

Little Chip ran up and threw his arms around me and begin to cry.

"I don't want Babby to go," he wailed.

"Don't worry, Chip. I'll be back in six days. Bye everyone. Love ya and I will call everyday."

I got into the car where the whole gang was waiting for me. Our teacher, Mrs. Bossart, her husband and two other teachers from our school would meet us at the airport.

"Abbbbbby, I can't believe this," Andrea chanted. "Me either. We are going to save sea life and have a great vacation." We drove to the big airport in Dallas and waited on our plane.

Now I know that Alison's mother is a movie star and rich, but we did not get to sit up front in first class but we sat in coach. This is where the rest of the common folk sit as well as a baby named Kinsey.

"Shut Up"

Alison, Alexis and I sat by each other on the plane while Anthony, Neils and Andrea sat across from us while Mrs. Bossart and the other teachers, Mrs. Gray and Mrs. Hill sat three rows behind me.

Since neither Alexis nor I can see the view anyway, we let Alison sit by the window.

Right in front of me was a baby named Kinsey.

I could first hear her gurgle to her young mother.

Her mother sounded really young and really annoyed at the baby before we took off. She put little Kinsey down and let her run up and down the aisle after we were way up in the air and got to take off our seatbelts.

"You stupid," she squawked and hit my leg.

"Who is that?" Alexis asked me.

"It's some annoying kid and she just hit my leg."

I guess Kinsey's mother heard me because she picked up Kinsey and plopped her down hard on the seat and said, "Well, Kinsey, the girls don't like you so leave them alone." With that smart retort, Kinsey let out a huge wail and woke the whole plane up.

She screamed some more and some more. We had been in the air for three hours and there wasn't a person on the plane who liked Kinsey. The whole back of the plane got quiet when a teenage boy screamed,

"Shut that kid up!"

At first I was glad that the jerk screamed at the baby and the mother, but then I could hear the mother crying softly. I felt so bad for her and her baby. After all, the baby was only probably two years old and the mother not much older than that maybe nineteen or twenty years old from the sound of her voice.

I tapped Mrs. Kinsey on the shoulder and asked her if I could play with Kinsey.

"Sure, I guess," she sniffed, so I took Kinsey and we played with music, sang songs quietly until she was fast asleep.

The rest of the time Kinsey slept in her mother's arms. Before our plane landed I felt a face close to mine,

"Thank you so much," Mrs. Kinsey said. "I don't know what I would have done without you."

Kinsey would not be the last sound of crying that I would hear on our trip.

"Waikiki"

After we got off of the plane we left the airport in a mini van. Mrs. Bossart, Mrs. Gray and Mrs. Hill were all organizing the eleven of us. Besides: Anthony, his twin brother, Aaron, Neils, Alison, Andrea, Alexis and me, there were four other kids: Scott, Claire, Keithia and Joey.

The next day was so much fun. Mrs. Bossart and our other chaperones took us to the Dole Plantation which is north of Honolulu.

"I really want to go to the beach in Waikiki," Alexis told Mrs. Bossart.

"We will go straight to the beach after we tour the northern shore and go on a really cool tour Mrs. Bossart replied.

We ate so much pineapple there at the Dole Plantation and everywhere else we went in Hawaii.

I was a little surprised at how chilly the air was up north in Honolulu, but from what I heard from our sighted friends was that the color of the water in Honolulu was the most incredible color of blue.

"Help me to understand what you're seeing," I asked Neils.

"Well, you see Abby," she continued, "You know the taste of a coconut slush that you love to drink or the coconut snow cone that you really like? That's the color of blue that I see when I look at the ocean water."

"Wow. Thanks, Neils."

Even though I have the best family and friends in the world, I still get frustrated with the sighted people because they forget that I am missing out on beautiful sights. I told my vision teacher, Ms. Ashley this one day.

"Abby, you need to politely remind them that you need to know what your surroundings look like. We sighted people sometimes forget to tell you because we can get caught up in what we see naturally."

"Thanks, Ms. Ashley," I had said.

So, everytime I hear the ooooooh, aaaaah, I ask my friends or family what in the heck is going on.

At the Dole Plantation I ate the most delicious pineapple shake. I mean it tasted so good that I drank it too fast and got a brain freeze.

"Ouch!" I Yelled.

"What's wrong, Abby," Andrea asked me.

"I drank that shake too fast because it was so good," I said.

"Abby, you always make me laugh," giggled Andrea.

We rode on a train that to Anthony, Alexis and me was kinda boring since we couldn't see what was going on, but we still had fun just riding on a mini train.

After we shopped in the gift shop, Mrs. Bossart told us to get ready to get back in the van.

I bought the cutest stuff doll named Bob who was a pineapple character, and I also bought the most adorable pineapple toothpick holders for my mom and Katy.

After we drove around up north we went back to the Hyatt Regency where we were staying and went to our rooms. "I can't wait to get out there and surf," squealed Neils.

"Me either," Andrea sparkled.

"I believe I am going to read my Braille mystery story and lay on the beach with our teachers," I said.

"I want to read, too," Alison echoed.

"To quote Jaxson," laughed Andrea, "I ain't never seen such a beautiful place."

We laughed and rode down in the elevator where we met the rest of the group. We walked across the street and onto the beach.

The smooth white sand felt so great on my tired feet. I could not wait to get in a recliner and read my Braille book.

"Come on, Abby," Alison yelled.

"Come out to the water. Anthony, Aaron, Neils and Andrea are surfing. I'll describe to you what is going on," she said. I wasn't ready for the ice cold water that hit my feet.

"WOW!" I screamed. "THIS IS FREEZING!"

Mr. and Mrs. Bossart, and our teachers Mrs. Gray and Mr. Orta laughed their heads off. I mean I could feel the really cool breeze but thought that Hawaii was always warm.

"Abby, we are visiting Hawaii during its rainier season. It's cooler but never cold here. It has a temperate temperature which means it pretty much stays the same all year round. Usually it's around 80 degrees. Today because of the earlier rain it is 75 degrees," Mrs. Bossart told me.

I was surprised that once I got into the water it did feel pretty good. I held onto Alison's hands and jumped over the really smooth and cool waves.

After we got tired, Alison and I went to our chairs under the umbrellas and read.

"Watch out, Anthony," I heard Andrea scream. "What's happening?" I asked Alison.

She just giggled and said that he just got wiped out by a big wave.

That night was really fun. We got dressed and headed to the night life along Waikiki beach. I wore my comfortable blue-green sundress and flip-flops and tied my long blonde hair up into a high ponytail.

"You always look so cute," Andrea told me.

"Thank you, Andrea. I am sure you do, too."

Later that night after a really fun day, we were all so exhausted that we dropped into bed.

That night I had a nightmare that something bad was going to happen to one of us. Someone else must have had the same dream because I heard a blood-curdling scream.

"Hanauma Bay"

"Who screamed," I yelled.

"You were sleeping so hard that I could hear you snoring really loud," laughed Alison.

"That was Andrea. She slipped in the bathtub because of all of the sand. She's okay. She just got a little scared."

We got ready for our field trip to one of the neatest places ever.

It is a nature preserve called Hanauma Bay.

We wore our bathing suits underneath our shorts and t-shirts and hoped in the van to a cool placed called Snorkel Bob's. Snorkel Bob's was a place where you rented your snorkel equipment. You got fins, a water vest, a snorkel mask and air tube.

Even though three of where blind, we would still enjoy snorkeling with our sighted friends.

Afterwards they could tell us what they saw while we were under the water.

When we drove up to Hanauma Bay and had to walk down a really steep hill while carrying our snorkeling equipment.

We arrived at Hanuama Bay, and they put us into groups and then we piled into one room to watch a film about preserve nature in the ocean.

"Pay close attention," Mrs. Bossart said. "This is where you're going to learn about protecting the coral reef, the sea turtles, and the beautiful fish. Our oceans are beautiful resources that we want to protect."

We all agreed, struggled to put on our equipment, held hands with our partners, and dove into the beautiful ocean.

I was with Mrs. Gray, Anthony was partner with Mrs. Bossart and Alexis was with Mr.

Bossart. It was such a great experience. I could feel the coral reef's rough edges while we swam under the top layer of the waves.

One fish came by me and I felt it brush past my leg. After about an hour of snorkeling, we ate ham and cheese sandwiches, chips and drank sodas.

"Okay everyone," Mrs. Bossart began. "Tell me what type of fish, coral and other sea life that you either saw or felt."

We discussed all types of wonderful sea life, discussed the film on preserve nature and went on a brief nature hike.

This trip was too good to be true. The beauty, the fun and nothing mysterious had happened. I had spoken too soon.

"Noelani and June Bug"

We went back to the hotel and rested before we would embark again on another adventure. It would be my first luau and I hoped not my last.

A luau is a Hawaiian feast with music, entertainment, dancing, singing and tons of fun. For the luau I bough a really great dress, it was a short black dress with a halter top which means the dress stays on because the top of the dress ties around my neck. I also wore some really cool black and white beads that I bought in Waikiki.

We all boarded a tour bus and met Cousin Pam.

Cousin Pam was our tour guide. She was hilarious.

She kept calling everyone and everything good-looking. She told us the name of our "good-looking" bus driver, Gus.

"Abby," Neils began.

"Be glad that you cannot see our good-looking bus driver, Gus. Girl, he ain't good-looking and weighs around four hundred pounds."

I laughed outloud until some rude woman told me to shhh.

"Whatever," I said under my breath.

When we got to the luau they had activities planned for everyone. They first handed us a beautiful lei made of orchid flowers that we wore around our neck.

We then got a fruit drink. Neils, Anthony, Aaron and I went on a canoe ride and then later made beautiful lei to go around our head.

The nice Hawaiian girl named Noelani showed me how to make a lei using a needle and thread.

It was the most relaxing thing to do.

"Can you see anything," asked Noelani sweetly.

"No, nothing," I said. "But being blind has never slowed me down from having fun," I giggled.

"I can see that," Noelani laughed.

Noelani took the whole gang and me to the beach and taught us how to hula dance.

"Whoa, you go, Alexis," laughed Andrea.

"Alexis has it down," Noelani told us.

We went to a really cool outside event where the hula girls and men danced and carried out a roasted pig to begin the celebration.

"Abby," Noelani said. "You must taste the pig," she beamed.

"Okay," I stuttered and was trying not to gag at the thought of Charlotte from Charlotte's Web.

I was pleasantly surprised when I tasted the pig.

It wasn't nearly as bad as I thought it would be, but I immediately spit out poi.

It tasted too much like paste. Noelani laughed and laughed at me.

"Abby, you brighten me up," she said.

"I will come back and join your group in a while, but now it is my time to dance."

"You're a dancer on the stage," I asked.

"Yes, Abby. I am a professional hula dancer.

Years ago, people told their story through dancing because not everyone spoke the same language. A god or goddess would dance, so it was considered a religious dance but is now entertainment."

When Noelani danced on the stage, Anthony and Aaron went crazy.

"You go, Girl," they screamed.

We laughed and cheered on our new and kind friend.

After Noelani danced, she told me every move that a handsome fire eater named June Bug was doing.

"Abby, I wish you could see June Bug," Neils said. "

"Does he look like one," I asked.

"Like one what?" Neils questioned.

"Like a June Bug," I said.

"Nooo, Girl, he looks like the king of the universe. He is so handsome with black hair, dark skin and big muscles."

The way that Noelani laughed at Neils and talked about June Bug I began to think that they were more than friends. Perhaps they were lovers.

"Missing"

Noelani and the gang and I walked around the luau and shopped. I got up my nerve and hesitantly asked her about her relationship with June Bug.

"Are you and June Bug going out?" I asked. There was a brief period of awkward silence and then she spoke.

"Yes, Abby, June Bug and I are going to married." "That's wonderful, Noelani," I shouted.

"Well, we have a few obstacles to overcome first, but I want to get married just the two of us by the beautiful ocean."

"That is so cool," I smiled.

Later that night I asked Neils what Noelani looked like.

"Oh, Abby, she is one of the most beautiful person that I have ever seen. She has really long black hair, dark skin and enormous gold colored eyes. She's Hawaiian but I believe she must be a mix of other races, too."

I knew that she must be beautiful, I thought.

Of course, anyone that was so kind and thoughtful to others was in my opinion, the most beautiful person anyway.

After the luau we got back on the good-looking bus with our good-looking cousins, Gus and Cousin Pam. I feel asleep on the way back whenever I felt a slight nudge on my arm.

"Hey, Honey it's time to wake up."

I realized the voice was not from my group but from the lady earlier on the bus who told me to be quiet. "

"Thank you," I told her.

"I was going to get you up," Alison smirked.

"That old grumpy woman must have felt bad for yelling at us earlier," Neils smurked.

Oh, well, I thought. This was the most wonderful trip ever and nothing could ruin it. At least that was what I thought until the next morning. I slept hard and had many fitful dreams. Dreams that begged me to pay attention.

"Abby, wake up," Neils begged.

"What time is it?" I asked.

"Abby," Neils continued, "Noelani and June Bug are missing."

"What?" I screamed. "How do you know?" I asked. "Well, while you and the other lazy bones were sleeping late, Mr. and Mrs. Bossart and I went downstairs for some breakfast and it's been splashed all over the news. 'Missing Hula Girl and Fire Eater'. The article stated that after the luau the two have vanished into thin air. Noelani's parents were so frightened when they did not hear from her, went over to her house and she was gone. Her purse, clothes and everything looked perfectly in place. Even her cell phone was lying on a table.The police tried to call June Bug and went over to his place, but it too was empty.

The whole gang and I went downstairs and moped.

"What could have happened to her?" asked Alison.

"I don't know but someone that nice would not leave without telling her parents and making them worry," I said.

"Children, there's nothing that we can do about that. I am sure that Noelani is safe and maybe forgot to tell her parents that she was going to be gone."

We knew that Mrs. Bossart did not believe that any more than we did, but she was making an attempt to make us feel better.

"Let's go back upstairs and get ready for the nature hike," Mrs. Bossart said.

We went grudgingly up the elevator, put on our jeans, t-shirts and tennis shoes and headed out for another surprise.

"Waterfalls"

We got back into the really silent van and headed to the nature resort where we would follow an ex-marine named Mike. Mike was a great guy, totally in great shape and expected the rest of us to also be an ex-marine. Okay, I am exaggerating because Mike was really patient with the blind kids while we tried to follow everyone up a really steep hill with our canes and a walking stick.

"Abby, let's fold up our canes and put them into our backpacks," Alexis said.

"Great idea," I said and told Anthony to do the same.

We walked, I huffed and puffed, swallowed a fly and slid down a mud bank. In other words, I was a total disaster. I finally told the others to go on without me.

"Don't worry, Abby, I'll stay with you," Neils said. Sometimes my friends can forget about me and my hardships being blind but most of the time they are very considerate and helpful.

"Thanks, Buddy," I said.

"Up ahead is one of the waterfalls, so let's walk a few more yard," Neils said.

"Great, but Neils, I need to sit for a few minutes. Go ahead and I will wait for you here. You'll just be a few feet ahead of me," I said. She agreed and I sat down on a big rock. I could hear some chickens running along our path. I was chuckling to myself whenever someone grabbed my mouth from behind and told me to not scream.

"Can You Keep a Secret?"

I wanted to scream and pass out until I heard the sweet voice of Noelani.

"Noelani, is that you?" I said with a relief.

"Yes, Abby. I am okay and so is June Bug."

"Did you know that the whole island is looking for you and afraid for your life?"

"Yes," was all she said.

"What's wrong Noelani?" I asked.

"Abby, I bonded with you and group the other night so much, so June Bug and I followed you back to the hotel and today on the nature hike. We want you to tell our parents and everyone else that we are okay but that we are going to married with or without their blessings."

So this is what the mystery was about. The two love birds wanted to be married but couldn't because of family problems.

"Why don't they want you two to be married if you are in love?" I asked.

"Because they say that since we are only nineteen years old that we should go to college and get married much later. We love each other too much to stay away from each other. My parents have money and June Bug is poor. My mother keeps telling me that I can do better than marrying a fire-eater poor man."

Just then the whole gang came back and saw Noelani. "Noelani" they all screamed. Everyone hugged her tightly.

"I want Abby to deliver this message to my parents and to the news," Noelani stated.

"I want the message to be that June Bug and I will hide out until we get their permission to marry.

If we do not receive their blessings then we will run away to the mainland and live there forever."

"Where is the mainland," asked Aaron.

"Aaron it is the United States. If they do not get permission and blessings to marry, then they will not have anything else to do with their families," Mrs. Bossart said.

I turned to say something to Noelani but just like before she vanished.

"The Families"

After the nature hike with ex-Marine, Mike, we went back to the hotel and began frantically looking for Noelani's family.

Mr. Bossart called the tour company for the luau who put us into contact with the family and the Hawaiian police.

We told Noelani's family and the police everything. Her mother was silent.

Here again was that awkward silence that made me terribly uncomfortable.

"Well, I am relieved that she is safe, but I feel that she is still too young to marry," her mother said stubbornly.

To our surprise Alexis spoke up, "Mrs., I do not mean to interfere, but the two of them are in love. You do not want to lose your daughter forever, do you? Simply give them your blessings and you will have your daughter return as well as a new son-in-law. Do you like June Bug," Alexis asked.

"Yes, he is a very nice young man, but he cannot support her breathing fire for the rest of his life."

"I know, but trust me there are more important things in life than money and fame," Alison said and told her the story of her family life.

After much talking and coaxing the families all agreed. We did however, have another problem, how did we find Noelani and June Bug to tell them the good news.

"They Said Yes!"

The next to the last day of the trip was really sad for all of us. We still had not located Noelani or June Bug, and we had to leave paradise within the next couple of days.

"I have a great idea," Anthony said aloud to everyone.

"Let's call the local news and newspaper. We can show them our pictures from the luau with Noelani and have them to send the message to her."

We cheered and agreed with Anthony.

Mr. Bossart found a news channel who ran a beautiful story on the two lovers and asked them to call home. The newspaper also ran a story with the headlines that said, "They Said Yes".

During the wee hours of the next morning, we heard from Noelani when she called the hotel and told us that we were invited to a Hawaiian wedding.

"The Wedding in Paradise"

We were so excited and could not wait to shop for wedding clothes. I bought a new long dress in an ivory color with sparkled sandals and a brand new purse that was created with the treasures from the ocean.

The wedding was the most wonderful affair.

We were all waiting on a beautiful isolated beach in the middle of nowhere. A beautiful long stretched limousine pulled up with a bride and groom who were madly in love.

"This is too much lovey stuff for me," Anthony and Aaron stated.

"Oh, come on Guys," Andrea said, "This is beautiful."

According to Mrs. Bossart the bride wore a long straight white dress that was strapless. She wore long diamond earrings and had her long beautiful dark hair pulled up on top of her hair.

June Bug was handsome in his Hawaiian white wedding shirt and khaki pants.

After traditional vows there was a Hawaiian blessing shouted over the couple while they placed orchid leis around each other.

We clapped and cheered for the new bride and groom.

After the wedding we went to a grand party at the hotel where we were staying. We ate and danced like crazy. Everyone freaked out whenever Anthony and I took the dance floor and danced all over the floor.

"You go, Anthony and Abby," the gang screamed.

Everyone was cheering and clapping for us.

When it was time for the bride to throw the bouquet, she threw it into the crowd and you'll never guess who caught it.

"It's mine," screamed Neils.

We laughed so hard.

"That means you have to be married next," I told her.

Neils immediately tossed the bouquet to Noelani's old aunt who had never been married.

"Oh thank you! It is finally my turn to be married," she squealed.

Before we knew it, we were packing to go home and very sad at the thought of leaving paradise.

A hui hou- "Until we meet again"- Abby